Hans Vater

At the Feet of Maharishi

My Time with the Master

'A fascinating book. Absolutely authentic and vividly told. As if you had been there yourself. I couldn't stop reading.' Michael Rabben

What is the inner makeup of a person who feels the urgent need to serve his spiritual master? When Hans Vater met Maharishi Mahesh Yogi in person, he soon was so attracted to his charisma that he did everything he could to follow him and be close to him. With relentless openness he describes his spiritual ups and downs from his time with Maharishi, how a very personal relationship with him developed, how he climbed up the stepladder to be Maharishis personal secretary and finally said farewell lovingly, so that he felt free to go his own way again.

Hans Vater received his Ph.D. under Carl Friedrich von Weizsäcker with a thesis on Plato's dialogue 'Parmenides'. In 1972, he was trained as a teacher of Transcendental Meditation by Maharishi Mahesh Yogi. From 1978 to 1981, he was Maharishi Mahesh Yogi's personal secretary. After a serious illness, he joined the 'Thousand Headed Purusha', a group of advanced TM practitioners. Since 2019, he lives in the spiritual community *'Yoga Vidya'* in Bad Meinberg, Germany.

Hans Vater

At the Feet of Maharishi

My Time with the Master

Alfa-Veda

Original title:
Zu Füßen Maharishis: Meine Zeit mit dem Meister
Copyright © 2019 Hans Vater

Translation: Anjali Mahaldar
Editor: Vernon Barnes
Proof reader: Jennifer Williams
Cover design and layout: Jan Müller
Photo on the back cover: Vernon Barnes

1st edition September 2020
Copyright © 2020 Alfa-Veda Verlag, Oebisfelde, Germany
www.alfa-veda.com

ISBN 978-3-945004-47-0

Contents

Prologue

It was on the morning of 31 October 2004. I slammed the trunk of my green Honda Civic, which, as always, rattled slightly. I got into the car and slowly drove past the entrance of the Ilse-Eickhoff-Academy in Bremen, where I had spent the last four and a half years.

No one was there to be seen; they were probably all 'in the program', as they said there, that is, in meditation. I looked at the dashboard: 10:04 AM. Actually it was only 9:04 AM, because last night the winter time had begun. My car was loaded with about half of my possessions. I had already brought a first load to my new domicile in Hamburg three days ago.

So, this was, I thought, the final farewell to the TM Movement to which I had dedicated my whole life since 1971. A period of about 33 years had come to an end.

I had learned TM, Transcendental Meditation, in November 1967, when I was studying philosophy in Hamburg with my supervisor Carl Friedrich von Weizsäcker. The encounter with TM at that time had initiated another farewell, namely the departure from a normal bourgeois academic career. For after a period of regular morning and evening meditations, I simply could no longer imagine spending my life with the theoretical analyses of old philosophical texts and academic debates.

So, soon after finishing my doctorate on Plato's 'Parmenides', I flew to Mallorca in the summer of 1971 to take a seven-month intensive course to become a Transcendental Meditation teacher. Meditation then determined my life for over 30 years. I became director of the TM Center in Munich, then regional coordinator and later director of the German TM Movement. Then I spent years in Seelisberg, Switzerland, in the international headquarters, at the feet of Maharishi, who had introduced Transcendental Meditation to the West.

The absolute highlight of my career was my two and a half years as a Personal Secretary to Maharishi. After that I was, for 17 years, a member of a group of Vedic[*1] monks called 'Purusha,'[*2] which Maharishi had founded. After I had left this monastic group in January 1999, I looked for a job in active life. By some coincidence I ended up as the administrative director of a small Ayurvedic[*3] chronic disease clinic that belonged to the TM movement.

This time also came to an end. The clinic was closed and I ended up in the Meditation Academy in Bremen. There I started to publish my esoteric knowledge and spiritual insights in book form. My first book was published in April 2003, the second one I had finished two weeks ago and sent out to publishers, just in time before my move.

It had been clear to me for some time that I no longer belonged to the Meditation Academy and the TM movement, and now an opportunity had arisen to move to Hamburg, only about 30 kilometers away from my birthplace Reinbek. Not that I was disappointed in TM. Not at all. I still consider this meditation a very, very good technique and feel deep gratitude towards Maharishi, who has supported me endlessly on my spiritual path.

Meeting with the Master

The first time I saw Maharishi was in autumn 1970 in Kössen, Tyrol, where he led a large course, a pre-teacher training. I arrived one day after the beginning of the course and parked my car on the square in front of the assembly hall, which was already full with about 1,500 people. At the far other end, on a stage, Maharishi was sitting, dressed in white, on a sofa covered in the same white. At that time, I knew nothing at all about how to behave towards an Indian master. I looked at him, certainly not very respectfully. Today it almost seems to me as if he had interrupted his speech for a second and looked at me briefly, like, 'Aha, he's here'. Nevertheless, I didn't become aware of that, if it was true at all at the time. I sat down in the back row and listened to his lecture.

In the following days, I learned that before each lecture there was a kind of welcome ritual, which I had missed on the first day, but which might have repulsed me a bit, especially since it was probably especially pronounced at the beginning of the course. Maharishi always arrived with a clear delay and was driven by a devotee to the back of the building, the stage entrance. In front of this entrance a long alley of devotees had formed, all with a flower or even a bouquet in their hands. For those who had experienced this before, they knew what happiness one felt when one could hand a flower to Maharishi and perhaps even receive a blessing, a look, or in exceptional cases, he even received a short greeting from him.

In the hall, the followers probably waited an hour or more. At some point, someone usually suggested that it was best to meditate now, and so there was an expectant yet peaceful silence. When Maharishi had finally made his way through the people waiting outside and entered the stage, everyone rose. Maharishi stood before the crowd, hands folded in greeting, and looked across the rows. In a flash, his eyes glided across all the faces. Then he said 'Jai Guru Dev',[4] which was answered by everyone with 'Jai Guru Dev'. the standard greeting in the TM movement.

He then sat down on the sofa, cross-legged under his white Indian dhoti,[*5] which always took some time. Meanwhile, some personal secretary or 'boy' pushed the low table in front of him, on which, besides flowers, there was usually a clock, which he apparently didn't pay much attention to. That's roughly how the greeting went several times a day, before each lecture. Later I realized that waiting for the Master was an important part of his training: focusing attention on him was supposed to raise the student's consciousness and help it to align with the enlightened consciousness of the Master.

In those early days, I watched Maharishi with interest. I had already noticed what a wonderful effect the mantra[*6] meditation he taught had. I thought, 'Whoever is able to teach such an amazing technique, he must have something special.' But now, that I experienced Maharishi live, my respect grew even more; I began to admire him more and more, even to love him.

One time, when the meeting was dissolved and he had asked everyone to leave, probably because he wanted to talk to some of them in person, I stood a bit cheeky, right in front of the stage and watched him from close up, watching the movements in the hall with a serious, almost stern look. What big eyes he had, infinitely intense and deep! For a fraction of a second, his gaze fell on me too, completely neutral, but then I knew that I shouldn't stand there and that my staring was not respectful.

What particularly impressed me, even inspired me when he spoke, was his quick-wittedness, especially when journalists came by and interviewed him. Maharishi seemed to have unlimited creativity. He could always give the question and the subject a completely unexpected twist that I would never have thought of, so that even the most aggressive questioners were disarmed. He also seemed to take pleasure in raising critical and stubborn questions from the ranks of the students. I remember that the owner of the satirical magazine 'Pardon', Johannes Nikel, who was himself a course participant, wanted to point out a weakness in his teaching. It was about the asanas, the yoga postures that were usually taught on the weekend residence courses as a support for meditation. Maharishi had a little brochure with asana instructions. In this brochure, it was recommended to say a short prayer before starting the exercises, which was also printed there. Nikel argued that TM was a purely scientific method and its whole teaching approach was purely factual; it was not appropriate for a prayer to be taught in a TM booklet. Maharishi just said, 'Oh, such a short prayer, only ten seconds!' Of course, that was not a counter-argument at all. Nikel replied that it was a matter of principle. However, Maharishi said after each argument, only, 'Ten seconds…ten seconds!' and almost dismissed the question. Nikel got more and more excited but Maharishi remained calm and repeated these two words each time.

Maharishi made a point of ensuring that his teachers had a dignified and correct appearance. He wanted to reach the ordinary people with his teaching. Since the Kössen course was a preparation for teacher training, he also mentioned a few times that the male teachers should not wear long hair. He did not want hippies in his movement. On this Course, there were indeed many of such styled young people, including me. Many were quite annoyed by the imposition of having to cut off their hair to become TM teachers. But since only a few had already decided to attend the actual teacher training course, they had not yet had to cut their hair, and the overall picture remained largely unchanged.

A little anecdote from those days illustrates the quick-wittedness of Maharishi's 'educational methods'. At that time, he sometimes gave advice about diet – later he avoided such things more and more in order not to distract from the core of his teaching. Among other things, he once said that brown, i. e. unpeeled rice would not be good, and one should eat white rice. Brown rice would be something for pigs. There was also opposition to this view. A long-haired boy stood up and argued that all the vitamins were in the husk and so on. Maharishi sat there for a while as if thinking. Then he said, 'Maybe it's also good for hippies.'

Before I came to Kössen, I had not yet had the intention of becoming a TM teacher. TM had proven to be very valuable for me – but that was it. In the course of the Course, however, I got more and more attuned to the path of Maharishi, found myself aligning to his teaching and becoming enthusiastic about it. Then there was a certain moment when Maharishi grabbed me (in my subjective feeling, I really felt this has happened). It was a full moon day. Maharishi had scheduled a moonlight ride with all the participants to a nearby small mountain. I knew this and had parked my VW right at the entrance of the parking lot to be able to drive directly behind Maharishi's car.

Nevertheless, when I waited there, my friend, Signe, who wanted to join me, was not there. I had to let almost all cars pass me. Finally, Signe came. We drove off, but were now, of course, far back in a long, long queue that almost reached from the valley to the top of the hill. At some point, halfway up the hill, we could not go on at all; we stood there, with cars behind us and in front of us. Very gradually, we reached the top of the hill, which was full of cars. Everything was quiet. Obviously, Maharishi had ordered that everyone should meditate. I leaned against a tire of my car to meditate, but then the meditation ended and the departure for the return journey began.

At one point, an alley of people had formed, several people deep, and the Bentley in which Maharishi was sitting slowly drove through these rows. I remember very clearly: Maharishi was sitting in the passenger seat and had rolled down the window. I stood in the second or third row and could hardly see him in the semi-darkness, only noticing him waving a flower back and forth to greet the row of people out of the window. As Maharishi passed by right at my height, I was suddenly gripped by such a feeling of happiness that I immediately knew, 'This is it; this is what I want to have always; I want to serve him, and that also means: I want to become a TM Teacher.' That was the turning point in my life.

It occurs to me at that moment that this situation was in some ways parallel to the situation in which Maharishi himself first met his Master, whom he called Guru Dev, and was 'grabbed' by him: Maharishi told on several occasions that in his youth he had always been in search of saints. Once he had heard about a very special saint, who was in the nearby mountain forests at the time. With a friend, he had hiked there in the dark night, found the house and had actually been admitted to the roof of the house where Guru Dev was apparently sitting in the dark. There was nothing to see, everyone was in meditation. Suddenly, for a short moment, a flash of light, like from a car far away fell on a figure sitting in an armchair: Guru Dev. At that moment, Maharishi knew, 'This is it, my search is over.' Not long ago, a friend told me that he heard Maharishi say in a small circle, 'There were no roads in the area, and therefore no cars. The short flash of light on Guru Dev must have had another source. Maybe the light came from inside him.'

So, when the Kössen course ended, I was determined to become a TM teacher. A girl I had met there urged me to sign up right away, just like she did herself. We were so enthusiastic! However, I thought that it would be better to finish my doctoral thesis first. Moreover, that was right. Otherwise, I would never have been able to do it again; and the doctor title later did me a lot of good in teaching.

On the last day of the course it was a sunny October day, there were moving farewell scenes. It seemed to me as if I had completed a whole life in that one month. And I guess it was. What had changed in me! Not only that I had fallen unhappily in love again from afar – with an English woman – no, my thinking and consciousness had become something completely different. I was a different person. My soul had gone through so many ups and downs, it was completely turned upside down.

When Maharishi was driven off by a devotee in his Mercedes, I tried to keep up a little bit more. However, apparently there was a flight to catch or another important appointment to keep. In any case, I could not keep up. Furthermore, I noticed that I had left my coat in my accommodation, a farm. I had to go back. I walked around the outskirts of the village, agitated and for a short time suffering from a severe depression.

At home, I then set about finishing my dissertation thesis. It was no longer important to me. But I thought, 'Just write down what you know now. It can't be more than rejected.'

My father died. I passed my doctorate. And a year later, I went back to Kössen for a similar course. This time I already volunteered as a helper. I arrived the day before the course started and helped check in. During the course I was then part of the 'Security' detail. I had to take turns standing at the door with others and make sure that only people with a badge[*7] came in, even if they were well-known meditators. In return, our security team always kept the first row directly at the feet of the Master free, a huge reward for such an easy job. At the beginning of the course, I still had long hair and my Che Guevara beard. I was still quite critical, no longer left wing, but still intellectual and scientific. Again, and again I stepped up to the microphone that was set up for the questioners in the front part of the central aisle. The old TM teachers who sat on stage with Maharishi probably already knew, 'Now it's that wild guy again with the long brown suede coat (it was just an imitation!), the hippie mane and the heady questions.' Nevertheless, Maharishi remained completely patient with me, even though he did not go to my level.

For example, once I asked him, 'You say that humanity is as old as creation. Yet geological and archaeological surveys have proven that humans have only existed for a few hundred thousand years.' – 'Oh!' Maharishi said. 'You find a bone every now and then, and then the bill is off by 50,000 years.' Of course, that was again no argument, but so the master let me run into the wall with my scientific head.

Once a special meeting was scheduled where everyone from his field of knowledge was to present parallels to Transcendental Meditation. I reported on Plato, with his term 'nous' – the direct insight in contrast to the insight of the mind. Maharishi praised me: 'You have a very good understanding of Transcendental Meditation.' I was surprised; I hadn't realized it at all.

Towards the end of the course I registered for TTC.[*8] In a special session, in front of the entire audience, each applicant had to hand in a written paper about any topic connected with Transcendental Meditation. Each one stepped onto the stage one by one. Maharishi sat on his sofa, looked at everyone with serious, inquiring but completely calm eyes and took notes. Afterwards, the others who had also been in front reported that it was impossible to look in Maharishi's eyes at that moment. Moreover, the same happened to me. We speculated that Maharishi might have looked at the aura and thus tested his eligibility for becoming a TM Teacher. In addition, indeed, at the end of the action, he mentioned that he had shortened a long procedure in this way. Nothing more, he said.

One day later, my friend Signe cut off my long hair.

Meditation Teacher Course

In October 1971, I took a flight, together with Rosita Wolf, the daughter of an older TM teacher, to Mallorca to do the TTC. Until the last moment, I could not believe it. In the airport bus on the runway in Mallorca Roswitha nudged me, 'Hans, we are here! We have made it!' After a longer taxi ride, we arrived in Cala Antena, at the south end of the island. We were actually there! The sun was warm; we waded in the shallow waters of the Mediterranean – pure bliss. Everything was lying in front of us.

In the Hotel Eugenia, everyone was allowed to request a room according to one's desire. I chose the number 723 on the seventh floor, with a balcony on the narrow side, facing the sea. I actually got it and during the next weeks was able to enjoy the sun rising above the sea every morning – for five months. It was an especially large room with a spacious bathroom that even had a window to the east. Unfortunately, due to its corner location and size, it was also very cold and draughty, only marble tiles, no carpet – and that was wintertime!

Below my room lived Christa L., whom I already knew from Munich. During the day, she heard me repeatedly as I moved and turned my meditation chair on the stone floor between 'rounds' (the individual meditation sections interrupted by asanas). Crazy and fanatical as I was then, I had the idea that I should always sit facing the sun when I meditated, because the master had once said that it was best to meditate facing East in the morning. So I concluded that I should follow the moving sun. Christa, below me, took the hourly disturbance with humor and patience.

That was not the only fanatical madness. I wanted to get the maximum out of it, to be enlightened by the end of the course if possible. For this, according to the theory, as much stress as possible had to be released, i. e., all the inner burdens of the psyche and thus of the nervous system. How to do that? By deep silence! That would regenerate and purify the nervous system.

The 'stress' – this word encompassed all genetically and biographically determined hardening of the psyche and the nervous system – was to dissolve as a result. So 'as much deep rest as possible' was the motto for me, and the deepest peace is achieved through Transcendental Meditation. This was proven by measurements of skin resistance, metabolic parameters and others. So, I decided to 'round' – to meditate – as much as I could in terms of time. Early in the morning, I got myself in my chair before the sun rose. I had given the armchair the right slant by placing a board, which I had picked up on the beach, under the front legs of the chair. This device made the moving of the chair, about every hour, even louder – I could not lift the chair because I would have lost the board.

The entire daily routine consisted, at least in the first months, almost only of 'rounds', interrupted by lunch and a short walk afterwards. Then it went on until dinner. After this, there was a 'lecture' by Maharishi in the great hall. But instead of sitting as far forward as possible to catch everything, I sat down in the last row, a thick blanket wrapped around me, and meditated even during the lecture.'[9] When the lecture or question time was over, I sat down again in my room in the meditation chair and continued meditating until I was to the point of exhaustion that put me to bed. But at dawn I was up again and meditated in the direction of the rising sun.

Already towards the end of the course, it became apparent that this strategy of fighting for quick enlightenment was not entirely without a downside. I felt I was losing the ground under my feet. I tried to counteract, but it was already too late. After the course, I noticed this. The stress release that had been set in motion by the intense meditation could not be stopped. This went on for several years. I found myself in a constant emotional turmoil: fears, anger, worries... the thoughts were constantly rattling. It was only by working very hard and meditating little – only ten minutes at a time – that I gradually got a grip on myself. But on the other hand, I realized: 'I am transformed. I am no longer the same as I was before. I am a new, softer, freer, more relaxed and loving person.' Many hardenings of the soul had been softened; knots had loosened. The purification had been worthwhile.

When I met my doctoral supervisor Weizsäcker again after the course, he no longer recognized me, even after I had already spoken a few sentences to him. He grabbed his head and thought hard. An assistant standing next to him jumped in and said, 'Yes, I didn't recognize Vater at first either.' Moreover, that was certainly not only because I had cut off my long hair.

Yes, it was a wild course and a wild experiment. I don't think even Maharishi had anticipated exactly how much 'stress' we still had inside of us. Even a highly enlightened master does not know everything and cannot foresee everything. Nevertheless, at that time, we believed that.

What made it difficult for me was that I was doing more than was 'allowed'. For example, Maharishi did not want us to fast. I did it anyway, secretly – because I wanted to purify myself even more. But that went very wrong. I had actually been aware of the risk: In fasting it is important is to return to normal diet very slowly. So, after a week of fasting I started to eat again, very carefully. However, I could not put together my diet freely; I had to eat what was offered. After three days, I had cucumber salad with grated hazelnuts. I thought, now, after three days, something like that should be okay again.

Nevertheless, that was a mistake. I got a terrible stomachache and it lasted for many weeks. Every little bit of food increased the pain. So I was forced to keep on dieting, and as a result, my system purified itself more and more. This in turn led to an increase in my appetite. This was not without unpleasant consequences. I developed an almost unbearable craving to eat. There was a constant inner struggle. On the one hand, there was this constant mental anguish, mostly in the heart area, which was only temporarily alleviated when something was running down my throat. On the other hand my reason, which said, 'Too much food is not good, pull yourself together!'

So, I tormented myself all the time and fought against myself all the time. It just got worse and worse. One day I went to Angelica. Angelica was almost something like Maharishi's secretary then. I asked her to give me the 'eating technique'. This was a special technique that Maharishi had developed for those who could not cope with their 'table-tendency', as he called it. Angelica instructed me in this technique. I felt a little bit guilty because neither she nor I had asked Maharishi if I could have it.

Anyway, I got this technique and I noticed how I relaxed during the instruction. I felt a great relief. Nevertheless, the effect in the next days, weeks and months was completely absurd: I could no longer fight my eating addiction. Almost without willpower, I gave in to my eating urge from then on. The stress really came out now. The agony in the heart area remained. The agony that was only masked in those moments when something viscous or mushy ran down my throat. Once I had started eating, I could not stop. The mental pain was just too strong. The consequence was that I always ate until I felt sick. It was a horrible time.

For my meditation, this was a catastrophe. Sitting upright with a proper meditation posture was out of the question. Most of the time I sat down on my bed, the pillow behind my back, leaning diagonally against the wall, my legs stretched out. I had once seen a picture of the fairy tale of the land of milk and honey, where people were completely overweight, obese, legs stretched out beside the rice mountain. I felt like that.

When I was once again completely desperate, an opportunity arose to tell Maharishi about my terrible situation. In the morning, I had eaten myself completely sick. In the evening, as usual, there was a lecture in the large cinema hall of Fiuggi Fonte.[*10] The hall was a little outside the village. The students, about 2,000 of them, were taken there by bus. They all sat in the endless rows of chairs, Maharishi, in white, on top of the stage.

As usual, he first asked for experiences. But this time, unlike as usual, he did not want to know the best experiences, but the worst. I recognized the opportunity; and although I was terribly embarrassed, I went forward to the microphone that was set up in front of the stage. I told him about my craving for food and that I no longer had the strength to resist it.

Somehow at that moment, probably because of Maharishi's presence, some distance from my suffering arose, and I said that it was probably 'unstressing'.[*11] He laughed and confirmed it. I felt better after that. On the way back, somebody offered me cookies, and again I could not say no, even though the stomachache from the morning was not over yet.So, those were the side effects of the course. I thought, 'Silly – this way I am going to screw up the whole course.' But it wasn't like that. The 'unstressing' was obviously the most important thing for Maharishi at first. He wanted our nervous system to cleanse and refine itself so that knowledge could flow through us more easily. So, I was just right with my 'stress release'; this was in alignment with the purpose of the course.

Maharishi spent very little time on knowledge in the first few months, and as I said, we met only once in the evening. If I had expected to gain deep insights from these lectures, I was disappointed. It was always about one topic: stress release, stress release and stress release again – and that was really not very interesting to me.

Maharishi usually began the lectures by asking about experiences in meditation. Many reported the most wonderful light appearances, infinity and eternity, absolute silence and so on, which made me feel envious. In most cases, however, Maharishi reacted with a wink, 'Yes, another such experience', everything was always just 'stress release'. It was almost tiring.

Probably Maharishi wanted us not to lose ourselves in experiences. We should come to know the 'Self', which is known to be beyond all experience, the basis of all experience. On the other hand, he also wanted to show us how we should later deal with any experience of meditation students. We should always look at the mechanism of stress release: Meditation gives deep peace; in this peace, the nervous system regenerates; and this in turn manifests itself on the mental level as thoughts, feelings, visions and the like.

Of course, there were also more interesting 'meetings' in between. After a few months, I got the courage to go to the microphone in front of the room and ask questions. Mostly they were quite critical. It seemed to me that the lesson we would later teach our students was not always completely honest. However, since I could not imagine that Maharishi could be dishonest at all, I thought it must be my fault that I did not understand the matter properly.

For example, Maharishi taught that in meditation the mind traces thoughts back to their source and then experiences them in pure form. Nevertheless, first of all, I had never had this experience myself, and secondly, it did not seem correct. In meditation, we might experience pure consciousness, but we did not experience it as the source of thought! As soon as we experienced a thought, it was always there! We never experienced its origin as pure Being, pure consciousness!

I don't remember how Maharishi reacted, but apparently he quickly grasped the pattern in my 'objections'. The pattern was, 'Can we honestly say that?' I remember a situation towards the end of the course when I noticed an ambiguity in a meeting and asked about it. Maharishi said to me, 'You always ask the same questions!' I said, 'No, I just thought of that.' Later I realized that he was right: It was again about honesty! At least he seemed to know me, despite the many other participants!

Actually, I had not only visited one TTC, but three TTCs in a row. Each course lasted ten weeks. You could, if you wanted, book several courses directly after each other. Then you did not take part in the actual meditation teacher training at the end of the first courses. One just 'rounded' while the others studied the teaching procedures. During the first course, all participants were concentrated in Cala Antena. During the second course, there were more students and at the same time, there was an advanced training course for people who were already TM teachers. So additional course hotels had to be opened in Cala Millor, about 20-30 kilometers away.

Those who had already taken part in the first course and wanted to continue were to move to the new course location, including me. I was very sorry about this, as I had such a nice room. All the 'movers' met in the lobby of the hotel. Maharishi himself was there and spoke to all those who were supposed to leave during the night. Someone regretted the move. Maharishi tried to make the new place palatable: It would be much quieter. I had to mention, at our current hotel, they had started to build a supermarket. However, since I lived at the front of the hotel, not directly across from the construction site, I thought that I would not be bothered that much. Finally, Maharishi asked, 'Who would like to stay here desperately?' I got up. When I looked around, I realized that I was the only one. Thereupon, I was allowed to stay in the old hotel I had stayed in, went up to my room and unpacked again.

I remember having a kind of waking sleep that night – maybe because I was a bit wired because of the 'move' and didn't sleep very deeply. I was sleeping, but I was conscious and saw a bright light in front of me all the time. Awake sleep was considered among us to be a good sign of approaching 'cosmic consciousness', a state in which one stays awake under all circumstances and watches oneself as a 'witness', even in deep sleep. Unfortunately, this did not happen to me again as clearly and for as long as that night. In the weeks that followed, Maharishi came to us only every second evening, the other evenings he was in Cala Millor. By the way, I heard that the students there were given earplugs on the second day because they were building there as well!

The building site in front of our hotel expanded more and more, also towards my end of the hotel and then became visible from my window. Especially the excavation of the foundation made a hellish noise, which was always repeated in three phases: First, holes were drilled into the limestone with pneumatic drills. Then the explosive charges that had been put in were detonated, and then the gravel loosened by the blasting was pushed away with huge bulldozers. After that, they drilled again, blasted and pushed it away and so on.

I also meditated with earplugs. Other students retreated to their inwardly located bathrooms. This was the way it was for these courses, if you wanted to save money and use the summer resorts in winter. Soon I regretted not having gone to Cala Millor. I spoke to a responsible person and asked if I could move after all. He said, 'What? You were the one who desperately wanted to stay here!' I had to surrender to my fate.

This second phase was a little lonelier, even sadder than the first one: Maharishi, as I said, did not come every day anymore. Christa no longer lived below me. Outside it was cold, and there was the somewhat bleak atmosphere of off-season resorts.

On 12 January 1972, there was a special festival. I hadn't noticed any preparations, but suddenly there were many more people there than usual and some of them came from far away. Many hundreds waited in the hall for Maharishi. However, I, along with many others, had placed myself in front of the hall, holding a flower in my hand, which I had picked in the field to hand to the Master. We formed a kind of disordered trellis. Maharishi arrived quite late as usual, walked through the line of people and received the flowers.

The unusual thing that happened to me was when he accepted my flower. He touched my hands slightly. Such a thing was considered a special blessing among the devotees; and I actually felt the loving energy of the Master flowing over me at the moment of touching. I was so happy that I did not mind not being let into the hall, which was completely overcrowded, waiting outside together with many others. However, we could listen to Maharishi's prodigious speech over loudspeakers. It was about the ceremonial Inauguration of the 'World Plan', according to which 3,600 'World Plan Centers' were to be established to teach TM. The new year – from 12 January to the next – was declared the '1st year of the World Plan' This started a tradition of having a special theme each year on January 12. The 12th of January became a kind of New Year celebration.

Only years later I learned that this day actually was Maharishi's birthday. He himself never spoke about it, but those who were close to him knew. As a monk he avoided as much as possible any reference to his biography – as it was the tradition of the Vedic[*1] culture: The enlightened one has no more history, because he is not an ego, he is only the all-encompassing cosmic consciousness. Biographical facts are irrelevant because they only refer to the person who turned out to be Maya – illusion. That is why no one ever knew Maharishi's age or details of his origin. Only the closest associates, who sometimes had to take his passport to the authorities, for example, knew the relevant facts.

After the second ten-week block of teacher training, we could not stay in Mallorca any longer, because the tourist season there was approaching. In a large meeting, we discussed together with Maharishi where we should go now. Many 'national leaders' praised holiday resorts in their countries, because everyone wanted to have the meeting in his home country. Everyone knew that a large group of TM meditators would bring an enormous Sattwa.[*12] to the country: namely, harmony, order in the collective consciousness and other positive trends. Finally the contract was awarded (in a manner similar to an auction) to the National

Director of Italy, who made Fiuggi palatable for us, as it was situated in the mountains near Rome. He had taken a close look at the site and conducted preliminary negotiations. The place seemed ideal, secluded and quiet, with countless hotels and pensions among the trees. We asked, 'Do the hotel rooms have carpets?' He said, 'The ones I saw, yes. But I haven't seen them all.'

I had thought that Maharishi had already decided in favor of Fiuggi before the meeting. Perhaps this was the only place that offered the opportunity to find suitable accommodations and meeting rooms for 2,000 participants. He had kept our minds distracted so that later disappointment was not blamed on him, since we had apparently made our own decisions.

The relocation was carried out by chartered aircraft on a March night. During the flight, we all meditated, because we knew that such a move was not 'completely without' consequence. When one has meditated so intensively for weeks, the whole system is completely softened, every little excitement and activity can set in motion an 'unstressing' experience, with emotions, excitement and mental imbalance.

From Rome, we went up into the mountains by bus. While the weather had been relatively mild in Mallorca and in Rome, it got colder and colder the higher we went. After a few hours, we arrived in Fiuggi about 3 o' clock in the morning. Immediately we were taken to our hotels and rooms; we could not take our luggage that had been transported as a bulk shipment; it would have taken too long to sort it out.

I came to a small, very simple hotel on a slope, and experienced an absolutely dreadful night: My room was small and narrow, the floor tiled, and no carpet! In the corner was a tiny toilet and a shower over the toilet bowl. Everything was freezing cold! The hotel had been empty all winter long and was completely chilled. Surely, the temperature had been below zero degrees Celsius until recently.

There was a shabby woolen blanket. I acquired a second one; but even that was not enough by far to provide sufficient warmth. My luggage with warm clothes and blankets was not available. I had once read about soldiers who were in Siberia. If they had one coat and two blankets, they did not put the coat on at night, but put it between the blankets, so that an insulating layer of air was created. Therefore, I did that with my thin imitation leather coat. I was too cold to meditate, and too cold to sleep; so, I lay on my back with my legs dressed, the two blankets plus the coat above me and trembled with cold and desolate misery. After the beautiful, big and relatively warm room in Mallorca and in my hypersensitive state, this situation was an absolute shock for me.

In addition, Fiuggi was obviously not at all secluded and quiet. It was a busy place. My hotel was located directly on the well-travelled road to Fiuggi Citta, the original mountain village above Fiuggi Fonte, as the spa was called, where we lived. The road was just a straight stretch of almost one-kilometer length, with a gradient of 8 to 10 percent.

Those who know the Italians will appreciate that they have a fondness for loud and fast cars. So, every quarter of an hour or more Italian sports cars thundered and roared up the hill, and even more often trucks that apparently supplied a construction site further up, noisily rumbled on. After my room in Mallorca with sea view and silence (at least at night), the new situation was hell for me. I decided, 'I can't stand it. I can't meditate here, I can't sleep and I can't live. I'll wait until morning, get my luggage and leave.'

However, when I searched and found my suitcases at the central place in front of the hotel where Maharishi lived, I had already calmed down a bit. Luckily, I hadn't found anyone to check out with that morning. I did not know how to get away from here. Finally, I found an official and at least told him that I wanted to move to another hotel. A week later, this wish was granted.

I was allowed to move to a hotel that was less noisy, but it was cold there too. My small electric heater – it was only a heating coil around a clay tube – didn't help much, because Italy had a different voltage than Spain. Besides, the fuses in the house blew at the slightest strain. (I heard that in other boarding houses students tried to warm their room by turning on their iron).

The last part of the course was about learning: what exactly to say in the information presentations and what to say during the actual TM course, what to say during checking and so on. The entire teaching system was already perfectly structured at that time; and we had to learn most of the teaching steps by heart. This proved useful afterwards. My first student, an elderly lady, noticed in me the confidence and precision I radiated in my instructions. For her it was obvious that I had many years of experience. I did not tell her that she was my first student.

Signe had entered the course at Fiuggi, and right up to the last teaching block we had crammed the teaching steps together and passed the examinations at the same time. Now came the great moment that we had been working for, for so long. Now we were to be made TM teachers by Maharishi himself and thus become representatives of the Holy Tradition. It seemed to be only a formality.

But no. Maharishi also used this situation to get rid of a lot of stress in our lives: He kept us in torture for days, making us wait and wait and wait. For me, as for many others, this went to the limit. Some of us had already booked our flights or made appointments at home. Nevertheless, that did not move the Master.

Finally, our group at least got into the lobby of the hotel where Maharishi was 'making teachers' in the basement. Again, we waited for hours. Finally, it was midnight and the 'initiation'/instruction was postponed to the next day. And the next day the same game started. Finally, our small group was let into the basement. We saw Maharishi on his sofa. We saw the small tables with the puja sets[*13] set up, where everyone would perform the small ceremony we had learned. This ceremony was performed before each TM instruction, and, according to the official version, was to remind the teacher that he always taught in the name and on behalf of the Holy Tradition. But, of course, it was more than just a reminder. It was a wonderful traditional ritual, during which, in front of the image of Guru Dev – Maharishi's Master as the representative of the Vedic 'Sacred Tradition' – one could see the Holy Tradition in a very special way, offering gifts such as water, light, fruits, flowers, rice and so on. This symbolic thanksgiving ceremony and offering to the Masters placed one in the timeless sacred tradition. At the end of this ceremony, when one bowed to the image, one felt the overwhelming presence of sacred powers. One actually felt like a representative of the tradition and was authorized to give the meditation mantra[*6] and the necessary meditation instructions. The instructions by the TM teacher, who was otherwise a very limited personality, gave a tremendous authority at that moment, providing the student a powerful impulse towards transcendence. This small Vedic[*1] ceremony was also performed before other important spiritual events, to invoke the blessings of the Holy Tradition, so to speak, and to give meaning to the event; and of course, this was also performed before the solemn initiation into the status of TM Teacher.

We waited as we sat on our chairs in a side area of the hall to step up to the tables and perform the Puja. However, just at that moment another group came into the room who had to speak to Maharishi. They were the leaders of the German TM movement. They sat down directly in front of him and started talking to him. We sat there, could not hear what was being said, feeling an increasing impatience and worry if we would even get a chance to speak. The meeting dragged on – until finally it was too late again. We should come back tomorrow.

The next morning our small group gathered again at the hotel. Again, we waited. Then it was said, 'Only those who had booked a very important appointment at home or already booked a flight could be made teachers that morning. The others should wait until the afternoon.' That was a test I did not pass. Signe said she had to leave today; I thought it was wrong, but she obviously had no problem with it.

I did not actually have an appointment, but I felt encouraged by her to lie as well. So, we came into the room and all performed our puja at the same time in front of Maharishi. However, I was so nervous because of my insincerity towards him, that at one point I didn't know what to do and I actually made a mistake. I hoped that Maharishi would not have noticed since everyone was singing and offering their gifts at the same time. However, after the puja Maharishi suddenly said that he would not continue until the afternoon and that we should come back then. I was so relieved; I went to him and gratefully gave him a flower.

In the afternoon the time had finally come. We did the puja in the presence of Maharishi, received the last, most important, very secret instructions via headphones, then went to Maharishi one by one and could speak a few words with him. First, he asked me, 'Are you leaving today?' I said 'yes', and I thought, 'If everything's done today, I can actually go.' I already had the train picked out. But honestly, it was not, because I did not have to leave the same day. Then he asked me if I really felt safe in all the steps of the teaching. Obviously, he had noticed my mistake in the morning. Nevertheless, I could say 'yes' with a clear conscience, because I was sure.

He accepted it. He opened a folder in front of my eyes, in which there was the picture of his Master Guru Dev. He pointed to the picture with his eyes and looked at me with an expectant smile, like a grandfather unpacking a present in front of his excited grandson. His gesture implied, 'Do you see the Divine Master here? Are you aware that from now on you teach always in the name of Guru Dev and in front of his image and thus be in the Holy Tradition?'

I must confess that I was a little surprised and unfocused. There was the faint idea, 'It's only a picture.' Nevertheless, I think he 'charged' the painting for me at that moment. It has been with me ever since. For decades, I had it standing on a small altar in my room; and I have always performed the initiation ceremony that precedes the introduction to TM in front of this very picture, as it was expected. The picture is alive; it is not just a piece of printed-paper. Guru Dev is actually present in it, overlooking my life from his place. I always feel him – as Maharishi's Master – as my own Master (this was later also suggested to me specifically by Maharishi. I will talk about that later), although I have never seen him in person.

So now, I was a TM teacher. The excitement was over, the tension released. I could have been totally happy and relieved now. However, I was not. It weighed on me that I had lied to the master. Surely, he had felt that. Moreover, indeed, when he later saw me from a distance, he looked away – whether because of my actual mistake or because I had a bad conscience and therefore did not want to look him in the eye, I do not know. Probably the latter. I actually stayed there the whole day because we were supposed to get some follow-up instructions. Later one of the officials saw me: 'You are still here!' I referred to the fact that we had to stay because of the additional instructions. That was accepted, but I was quite embarrassed. The next morning, I went down to Rome in a crammed train and then by express train to Munich.

Back in Germany

In Germany, like many others, I then began to put what I had learned into practice: I organized lectures, introductions, courses. In the beginning, I was not very successful. There were simply too many TM teachers and too few who wanted to learn TM.

I started my TM teaching work in my Reinbek home, where I visited my mother. Within a few weeks, I had only three initiations. Then the opportunity arose to move to the newly founded TM Center in Harlaching, one of the best residential areas in Munich. Here I was very happy, but even here the courses and introductions were not enough to keep me financially afloat. I was about to give up my dream of teaching TM full-time. I had this dream not only because the initiations and all the work teaching TM was connected with enormous feelings of happiness, but also because Maharishi had explained to us that it was best for one's own evolution and enlightenment to concentrate completely on teaching Transcendental Meditation.

After a few months in Harlaching, a further training course was announced, which all TM teachers should complete as soon as possible: The course in the 'Science of Creative Intelligence' – SCI. The SCI Course was to give TM a scientific basis to satisfy the intellect of the more western-minded people. It was an explanation of Transcendental Meditation in academic terms: 33 video lectures by Maharishi, coupled with written questions and answers.

Such a course was now supposed to be attended by everyone, both TM teachers and aspirants for later TTCs. Responsible as I was, I signed up immediately. The course for the Germans took place in Semmering in Austria. It was led by Peter H. Peter was a composer of electronic music, TM teacher and recently chairman of the youth organization WYMS (World Youth Meditation Society) which he founded. Peter was a very unusual and extreme personality. Until then I had never met anyone – except Maharishi himself – who had such nerves of steel and was so independent of the opinions of others. He had no fear of rejection, embarrassment or the like. As a TM teacher he had already been extremely successful and had brought thousands of young people to meditate. (However, due to some reputation-damaging escapades, Maharishi soon revoked his TM teaching license and that of WYMS. His idiosyncratic style was permanently incompatible with the TM movement).

Peter had a staff of devoted young men around him. When he appeared in public, he walked like a power charge: usually two to four of his men walked diagonally behind him – slightly staged like an arrowhead. His face was by no means hard or aggressive, but quite natural and relaxed; but with a mine of a certain invincibility, so that one knew: If I resist him, he will finish me.

His people, most of whom were younger than him, obeyed him to the letter. He called them by their last names, and so they had to call him – and each other, by last names, although they lived together as a group in rooms with bunk beds for years. They always wore suits, usually dark blue with a red tie. Peter wanted his WYMS to be an established and reputable business organization, which in his opinion meant that the members had to be very formal with each other.

I felt somehow uneasy with Peter from the beginning. On the other hand, his course management was impeccable and very effective. I myself was, as always, one hundred percent on the job, and I even borrowed, after the SCI lessons, the written course materials from the course leader in order to study it more intensively.

I also offered to translate the texts into German to assimilate them even more. Peter liked this and after the first course, he invited me to stay for the second month, which followed on from the first, and to continue translating the materials for free board and lodging. And so, I stayed there during the second and also the third course. At the end of the series of three courses, I even moved with the WYMS to their headquarters in Kassel and became a recognized member of the staff.

But I never really felt at home. I was constantly afraid of doing something wrong or not quite on the ideological line. On the other hand, I benefited from Peter's leadership style. His main concern was to develop the feeling in us that we could achieve anything. In addition, indeed, he gradually built me up into an effective leader. I am still grateful to him for that. How else could I have managed all the tasks ahead of me?

Soon after moving to Kassel, TM teachers were recruited for all cities to found a local WYMS-center together with young TM meditators. When I realized that this was also applicable for Munich, I applied for this job and got it.

Therefore, I became the director of the Munich TM Center and was able to put into practice what I had learned from Peter – but somewhat differently than Peter had imagined. In my new position, I could not achieve anything using power or authority, because all the helpers were volunteers. We could not pay salaries; there was no money for that. Everyone had to enjoy the job and feel that he was doing something meaningful for his own evolution and for the world. If someone felt he was pushed too hard, he just did not come back. This was a good lesson for me. Therefore, I had to learn to adjust to different personalities and gently channel their existing commitment into the right projects.

To my own surprise, I obviously had good organizational skills. That was amazing, since before I had only studied philosophy and worked on texts. Soon my TM Center was one of the most successful in Germany. This was mainly due to the fact that there was almost no rivalry between the TM-teachers regarding the initiations. Everyone got his share of initiations, even if he was not such a good speaker. The best speakers shared the initiations with them.

After some time, it happened that I also became the coordinator of Southern Germany, and now I had to visit other places in the area to get the Centers going. That was a strenuous phase. I got very little time to sleep. I meditated regularly, but only for a short time each time. My last thought in the evenings was 'What else can I do to keep our Center afloat and remain a full-time teacher?' And also, my first thought after a short sleep the next morning went again towards Center activities and TM advertising. Very soon, I was burnt-out and exhausted. I had probably neglected the balance between rest and activity mentioned in the SCI course too much.

Interlude in Seelisberg

One day I took the opportunity to go to Seelisberg, together with a friend, who was also a TM teacher. Seelisberg had our International Administration Center, where Maharishi lived at that time. Seelisberg is a small tourist town in Switzerland, situated about 800 meters above sea level, directly above the famous 'Rütli' at Lake Lucerne, where the Swiss Confederation had been founded some hundred years ago. The TM Movement had bought two old spa hotels, 'Sonnenberg' and 'Kulm', which were connected by an overhead walkway bridge over the road. When I arrived there, sniffing the light and fresh air and watching the busy back and forth movement of the many young TM people working there on the 'Staff'. I knew immediately: 'This is where I want to stay'. I wasn't even registered, but I decided to give it a try. I found someone in charge of the construction department, Bernd Metzner. Bernd knew me, and after some hesitation, he said, 'Okay, you can work with the painters.'

The Hotel Sonnenberg was just being completely renovated and rebuilt, and many meditators took the opportunity to help out, in order to be close to Maharishi. Painting was not really my thing, but I was glad to be able to stay. I got a small room and the next morning after meditation, I started to trowel off holes in the walls and paint them afterwards.

As I had already guessed, I did not enjoy this particular work, and after two days, I tried to get into the carpentry and joinery department. That suited me more, because my father had also done carpentry work as a glider pilot. He had even made some furniture for us. I could not do that, but my father had at least taught me how to hold a hammer properly and how to hammer in nails. I was actually assigned to the carpenters' foreman, Helmut. Over the next few weeks our group tore the connecting doors out of the suites in the Sonnenberg, closed the walls with sheet rock, and installed a shower in each room – not prefabricated, but properly with wooden walls and shower trays mounted on tar paper – many of which later leaked, as I heard.

I learned the job eagerly and quickly, as I had previous experience, and became one of Helmut's favorites; which proved useful as the staff was soon reduced and most carpenters, including skilled workers, were sent home. But I was allowed to stay and could continue to hammer around the house.

This was a wonderful time, especially since Maharishi personally watched the progress of the work at irregular intervals. He enjoyed such activities. He sometimes stepped unexpectedly into a room where I was perhaps just lying under a shelf, hammering nails. I would jump up and put my hands together in greeting. Maharishi answered the greeting and smiled affectionately amused. That was a happy experience every time. In the evenings, we from the building staff were allowed to sit in the large, unfinished 'lecture hall' when Maharishi gave lectures or met with individual groups to plan the expansion of TM or to work through any texts. It was paradise for me.

One morning I had the opportunity to listen to a very interesting conversation between Maharishi and a guest he met in the empty lecture hall. I do not remember how it happened that I was allowed to hang around there during working hours. Anyway, from one of the back rows of chairs I could listen to Maharishi talking with a young TM teacher from France up on the stage. He had come to tell Maharishi about a project that he himself had started. He wanted to build a meditation academy in the south of France, discuss details with Maharishi, and get blessings for the project.

Surprisingly, Maharishi did not like the idea; he preferred to use the young man for another project abroad. The TM teacher could not understand this at all. Such good land! Such a building opportunity! This could only be useful to the TM Movement! However, Maharishi could not be convinced. After all, the man even argued that he knew that God wanted this project. Maharishi said in an ironic tone of voice, 'You know God. You know God.' Finally, the man left the hall unwillingly and defiantly.

I had not experienced anything like this in a long time. After all, we TM teachers had learned from our long association with Maharishi that it was best for one's own evolution – as one had an enlightened Master – to follow him in every detail, in order to adapt to his consciousness. This was the path of enlightenment that Maharishi himself had taken with his

Master Guru Dev and which was anchored in the Vedic[*1] tradition. The young Frenchman had obviously not been aware of this. He had put his own small mind above the wisdom of the Master. That I was allowed to be present at this conversation had certainly been arranged from above so that I would receive a lesson.

As much as I enjoyed the work and the whole situation in Seelisberg, I suddenly decided one day to return to Munich. Moreover, this is what happened. Every morning there was a puja for the staff, the small ceremony that is usually done before the TM instruction. The few TM teachers in the staff took turns in this task. One day it was my turn. During the ceremony I was reminded from inside that my task was actually teaching TM and not doing carpentry. I also became aware that I was needed in the Munich Center, which would probably fail without me. An hour later I had signed off with Helmut – who of course wasn't too happy about that, he had just sent most of the other employees home – and I drove back to Munich. That was after almost exactly six weeks, the time normally taken for an ATR course.[*14] Back at the TM Center, I first had to get thing going again.

In autumn 1973, I took the chance to participate in the first regular ATR course, which however lasted only two weeks. It took place in Weggis at Lake Lucerne in Switzerland. I remember that during the video lessons I sat in the background of the room and stringed corals on gold wire to make a 'mala' (necklace). Otherwise, I did a lot of nonsense together with Reinhard B. (who was to replace me as Maharishi's secretary years later). The course was enormously relaxing.

Building up a new center

In those years, the center flourished more and more; the activities multiplied. One day one of the younger TM teachers came to me and said, 'Hans, our Center is too big and too expensive, we can't afford it anymore. We have to move to a smaller one.' I said to him, 'On the contrary, our center is too small; we need a bigger one!'

And so, that was the situation. We didn't have enough rooms. In a meeting I suggested to the other TM teachers, we were almost twenty at the time, I think – that we should look for a new Center. And so, we did. We proceeded in a special way, which I had learned from Wilfried Schoof. This North German TM teacher had told the group on my ATR course how he had found a wonderful, almost ideal Center in Kiel at the most favorable conditions.

He had proceeded as follows: He had walked again and again with a group of positive-minded TM meditators and teachers through the best areas of Kiel – where they would have loved to see the Center most, if money and other restrictions had not played a role. Together – that was important – they had looked at the most beautiful houses and imagined what it would be like to have a Center there. At the end they had three houses on their shortlist, one of them an absolute favorite – all that without any feasibility considerations!

Only then did they place an advertisement in the newspaper. That same weekend, however, an offer for sale appeared for the very house they had chosen. In addition, the owner of the house also responded to their own ad. After short negotiations, the deal was perfect and they got the absolutely ideal Centre at an affordable rent.

The 'support of nature' continued. One meditator donated beautiful furniture, another, a carpet dealer, made his most beautiful Persian carpets available gratis as an exhibition and so on. All these successes seemed to have resulted from a group of like-minded people thinking in the same direction and actively looking at the objects on site. Thus, the attention was channeled in such a way that the wishes came true in an unexpected way.

I had remembered this report of Wilfried Schoof and now proposed a similar procedure in Munich. Soon afterwards, we were seen strolling together through the streets of the Munich university quarter, looking at the most beautiful houses. It took a little longer than in Kiel, and we didn't find any houses in exactly the same streets we had wanted; but then suddenly one appeared that was perhaps even more convenient.

Then came true 'support from nature'! The owner had three apartments for rent in this house, one large and one small on the ground floor and another large on the first floor. He absolutely wanted to sign us – as he saw that we were an offshoot of an American private university, as it was written on my business card. I was only interested in the two large apartments; which we really could make something out of; each had an almost hall-like large room and many small rooms suitable for offices. He said, 'Why don't you take the small apartment as well?' I said, 'We don't really need those.' 'Alright', he jerked himself. 'I'll give you all three apartments together, for a square meter price of only 10 DM.' That was really very inexpensive, and so I agreed. Later it turned out that the small apartment was extremely useful for us: we could use the two extra rooms as offices and also the small kitchen, where our group had lunch together almost every day.

But we were not only supported with the rent but also with many other things: When this young TM-teacher from our team, who was an architect, visited the apartments with me and the landlord, the latter let himself be carried away with many promises of possible structural changes and renovations, which he then arranged.

In September, we were able take over the apartment, or was it already October? This is relevant because new heating was installed a little later. So, we froze terribly at first, while we were still furnishing the apartment. For me it was a difficult time. It was essential that we only had volunteer helpers. But who wanted to work in cold and not yet 'meditated' rooms? People just didn't come, or at least hardly ever came.

Anyone who has to furnish an apartment with almost no money knows what small and big problems can arise. In addition, at the same time, of course, many other projects were pressing, because after all, all other TM-related activities had to be maintained! The whole thing grew so over my head that I would have loved to run away screaming almost every day (that is not an exaggeration!).

Luckily, I stayed, and one day we celebrated the official inauguration, which I used for publicity: Among other things, we had sent out a very nice newsletter with floor plans of the new center and pictures of the premises. Therefore, our hall was well filled for the opening; there were even some celebrities from out of town. But before that, I had achieved a small feat, because of which I am still proud of my trust in nature at that time. Our old chairs were no longer suitable for the new apartment. We needed new ones; there was no doubt in my mind about that. But we had no money! Moreover, chairs were not cheap at that time either. Nevertheless, I had brochures from furniture companies sent to me, and we finally chose a nice chair for 80 DM. I ordered 100 pieces. That seemed to be on the edge of irresponsibility. But I knew: 'It simply has to be!' I was hoping for 'Nature's support'.

The chairs arrived the day before the opening. We unpacked them and set them up. They were very beautiful. The invoice came with a 30-day payment term; unfortunately, we had to do without the discount. Then the deadline was approaching. We still had no money. On a Monday, we had to pay the bill. The weekend before, we had a lot of initiations – I think there were 16 – and at the same time a well-attended weekend 'deepening'-course was running, which brought us a pleasantly large amount of money. On Sunday evening, I counted the money in the cash register. It was just over 8,000 DM! So, I went to the bank on Monday morning and transferred the money for the chairs as if nothing had happened.

The building up of the new center exhausted me, and one day I decided to go to Arosa for a few days, where Maharishi was staying. I took a young TM-teacher with me. Arriving in Arosa, we rented a room and the next morning we drove up to the Hotel Prätschli, where Maharishi resided.

At that time, it was still possible at times to get into his hotel just like that. So, we went inside and walked straight to the main hall where Maharishi actually sat, surrounded by about 30 to 50 people. Some plans were being made. We could just sit there. What a relief to sit near Maharishi and relax! It was a gift and a reward for my difficult times in Munich. During a break, I gave Maharishi a flower and he looked at me lovingly and intensely. He had surely noticed how exhausted I was. Immediately afterwards I felt strength again.

Inauguration of the 'Dawn of the Age of Enlightenment'

Over New Year 1974/1975 I again visited an ATR course. Shortly before January 12th, it became known on this Course that Maharishi wanted to proclaim the 'Dawn of the Age of Enlightenment' and inaugurate it solemnly on Lake Lucerne. We were very excited and hoped, since Maharishi had to have the vision and perhaps even could turn the fate of the world, for a wonderful turnaround of the whole world events. Our Course was at Brunnen; Maharishi lived in Vitznau, also on the lake, where he was to board the large flagship 'Gotthard' to perform the solemn inauguration on the water. We students were to be packed into smaller pleasure boats and then meet Maharishi's ship on the lake. Of course, we would have preferred to be on his ship, but it was much too small for all the people who were to join from the various courses in Switzerland and for the many guests from abroad. Nevertheless, we were all very excited, even if some of us had certain worries about the abrupt interruption of our long meditation rounds.

When I stepped out of our course-hotel, Wolfgang approached me – the same TM teacher who was later to place me in the secretarial position to Maharishi – and asked me if I wanted to go with him in his car to Vitznau. Well, ok. I would miss a boat trip, but who knows… And I did not want to turn him down. When I got out of the car in Vitznau, our national director in Germany, Mr. Ritterstaedt, approached me, who for some, probably karmic, reason held me in high esteem, and called: 'Dr. Vater' (he always addressed me like that), 'I have reserved a ticket for you for Maharishi's ship! You can pick it up at the information tent.' Unbelievable! So, I rushed to the tent and got my ticket for the flagship Gotthard, while all the other students had to stay on their little boats.

The 'Gotthard' had two decks. The upper one, on which Maharishi would be, was only allowed for celebrities and invited guests. Nevertheless, I went up the stairs. At the top was Peter S. As a door checker, whom I had only seen a few times, but who was known to me as a successful TM teacher, and who probably had some respect for my doctoral degree. He said, 'Ah, Dr. Vater, yes please, you can go in.' This is how I actually entered the inner sanctum.

The rows of chairs had already been placed in a semicircle around the stage with Maharishi's sofa, but they were still empty. I thought, 'I'm not going to be allowed to sit in the front row.' So, I sat down in the second, right at the edge. Since I was still 'rounding (as they said in our movement) and knew that one could not suddenly reduce the meditation times without causing stress to his nervous system, I closed my eyes and started to meditate. Soon the rows filled up; and then I heard an usher come in and send almost all the people away. The first rows were reserved for very special guests. However, since I was immersed in meditation, he left me alone. Therefore, I ended up staying in the second row, among all the celebrities and close to Maharishi, for most of the hours of the ceremony! At one time, there was a longer break: the ship docked in Vitznau; Maharishi went ashore to his hotel. When he returned, I stood in the lower entrance area of the ship with many other admirers to present him with a flower. When he accepted it, he lightly touched my hands. When I wanted to go back upstairs to the upper deck, another 'door checker' was standing there and would not let me in. However, that did not bother me anymore, for I was so full of all the blessings I had received. And so, I enjoyed walking around the ship and talking to friends who had come from Germany. When after some time I felt like going into Maharishi's hall again, someone else was at the door again – who let me in promptly. The whole day, the whole 'Inauguration of the Dawn of the Age of Enlightenment', was for me a string of pearls of blessings and support.

The dream of Brazil

In final phase of this ATR course, I had applied for a new project called 'Associate 108'. Small groups of strong TM teachers were to promote or build up the TM movement in various countries, including Brazil. Brazil! My old longing for an exotic and very different kind of free life came across powerfully! Therefore, I applied for Brazil. Everything looked very good. There was already a partner who knew the country, spoke Portuguese and with whom I got along well. The leaders of the whole project wanted me very much. There was only one little thing missing, and that was Maharishi's approval.

The leaders tried repeatedly to get me near Maharishi so that they could ask him in my presence. One time I was even allowed to go on a small pleasure boat on which Maharishi was cruising on the lake with the participants of a very special course. I enjoyed the trip and basked in Maharishi's presence. It was interesting that during this trip, he repeatedly pointed out beautiful pieces of land on the shore that seemed ideal for the construction of a TM Academy. I thought, 'Aha, he wants to draw attention to these lands, so that through the desiring power of these advanced and highly developed TM teachers an academy could manifest there later on.' But this never happened.

As nice as the drive was, I could not get near Maharishi. After docking, he immediately retired to his hotel. Finally, it was already the day of my departure, a meeting finally took place. By chance, I was standing in front of the Park hotel in Vitznau when Maharishi came along in a car. When he entered the building, I walked towards him from the side, put my hands together and said, 'Maharishi, I have a strong desire to go to Brazil.' Maharishi, moving on, asked, 'Do you speak Portuguese?' I answered somewhat hastily, 'No, but I learn languages very quickly.' He already stopped listening and turned to another man who was walking on the other side and also wanted to ask something. During the long walk through the corridor, he did not pay attention to me anymore and disappeared into a room where he wanted to discuss some plans with staff members. I waited impatiently outside his door for a while, hoping to get an okay after the meeting. But then it dawned on me that I had already received the answer. It was 'No.' That was the end of my Brazilian dream. I drove back to Munich, still quite disappointed and also a little ashamed. During the drive, I suddenly realized that I was looking forward to Munich again. By the way, since that day my longing for Brazil has never come back. Moreover, at the end of 1975 I thought, 'How good that I stayed in Europe,' because of the Center, because of my mother, and because many beautiful things that happened for me that year. Among other things, I received a special, very effective additional technique at the next ATR. I had closer contact with Maharishi, and I was effortlessly led away from Munich and into new, larger areas of activity.

Inauguration in Munich

In the early summer of 1975, Maharishi personally came to Munich to inaugurate the Dawn of the Age of Enlightenment in a very grand way. Munich was one of the four German cities, along with Düsseldorf, Hamburg, and Berlin, that he wanted to visit on a world tour. We decided to make the visit as great as possible in the spirit and style of Maharishi.

So, first of all, we had to decide which hall to rent. In the ideal scale of about 2,000 seats that we imagined, there was none. The next smaller one was much too small and the next bigger one would have been the Six-Day-Racing Hall in the Olympic area, with 12,000 seats! With all the enthusiasm and optimism, we could not have expected so many spectators after all. In the end we took all our courage and rented half of the Olympic Hall – you could lower a wall or curtain in the middle. 6.000 visitors! I wondered whether we could drum up nearly that many people. In any case, it was quite a risk – especially a financial one, because this half of the hall cost 50,000 DM for the evening! And that was just the hall, not to mention decoration, advertising, Maharishi's accommodation and so on! We dared to do it anyway, but we also knew; 'Now we have to go to great lengths.'

And we did. Everyone cooperated, some of them to the point of exhaustion. For nights on end, our teams of helpers raced through the city, posting posters in the most impossible, usually forbidden places. As usual, we had to fight for the places with other spiritual and non-spiritual Movements, which also put up illegal posters. As a further advertising measure, we dug out our old card indexes and wrote to everyone who had ever been introduced to TM. – There were thousands of them: 'You should take this unique opportunity to see Maharishi in person'. I sat at the Center for several nights personally signing all these letters until my hand hurt. Eventually, I wrote my signature on Rhena index cards, which were then printed on several stacks of letters before the helpers bagged and stamped them.

During these weeks, I continued to travel around the southern German cities and promoted the Munich event. Finally, the big day came. It was wonderful sunny weather. Maharishi was expected to arrive at 11 o' clock with a private plane from Düsseldorf, the first stop of the trip, and then be driven to his hotel where he wanted to meet our team before the event. I already suspected that he would not be on time as usual. Therefore, we used the morning hours to finish the still urgent preparations in the Center. On the other hand, I did not want to miss Maharishi when he would arrive at the far away airport. So, I called his hotel in Düsseldorf around 11 am to check with the reception if he had already left. The woman at the reception asked: 'Who?' I said, 'The Indian!' 'Oh, I see. One moment, please…' – and she'd already connected me! Maharishi himself picked up the phone. Of course, I was terribly embarrassed. I didn't want to disturb Maharishi. Who was I? A small Center manager. It was more or less the feeling as if I suddenly talked to God personally! I stammered my apology and said I was calling from Munich and just wanted to know when he was leaving in Düsseldorf. He said, 'Ten minutes'. 'Thank you very much! Jai Guru Dev'.[4] He hung up. Now we could calculate when he would arrive in Munich.

When we arrived at the airport hall, hundreds of meditators were already waiting there and we sat down with them. After a few hours, I thought I could have used the time for the other work. But Maharishi was like that. Wherever possible, he kept his followers waiting. The sense behind this was often very clear: The inner tension was high when the attention was focused on the Master! It was an evolutionary leap every time!

Finally, we somehow got to know that his private plane was approaching the airport. Now it happened by chance that one of the older TM teachers, Adolf Beck, was employed as a customs officer at Munich airport. He was allowed to drive his car onto the runway. He took me with him so that we could receive the master right at the airplane.

I remember that I made an embarrassing little mistake there: When Maharishi appeared in the door of the plane; both Adolf and I wanted to give him a flower each. I pushed forward a little to show I am the leader and main organizer here. Adolf, however, was one of the very early meditators who had already attended Maharishi's first courses in Germany and knew Maharishi well. He deserved much more respect than I did. Promptly

Maharishi took his flower first, although he had kept himself modestly in the second row. Well, that was educationally valuable for me.

In the arrival hall, all the meditators crowded around Maharishi to give him flowers and receive his blessing. Then we went to his hotel where he received our center team right in the meeting room of his suite. We discussed the activities of the Munich Center. Back in the city, there was an extreme amount of work to do until the evening.

This was probably the first day since I learned TM that I did not get to meditate. I whirled around everywhere to oversee all the preparations. The time of the event was approaching. How many people would come? The visitors were very slow to arrive. Many people had heard of Maharishi, but for whom did his coming matter so much? It eventually became apparent that we would have about 3,000 attendees. Therefore, the hall would be half-full.

At this point, I went on stage and invited all those sitting in the tiers at the side to come to the more expensive seats in the stalls. (The next day the newspaper said that someone from the Movement had 'whipped' the people into occupying the front rows). In this way, the parquet was practically completely filled. We switched off the spotlights that were directed at the tiers; so, it looked as if the whole hall was full. Finally, Maharishi came on stage from behind and sat down on the white-covered sofa under the large golden letters on the purple dividing curtain: 'Inauguration of the Dawn of the Age of Enlightenment.' He closed his eyes and immersed himself in silence.

Normally, at every lecture in whatever place, Maharishi sat in front of a picture of his Master Guru Dev. We had been sent a large picture from the headquarters especially for this event, but unfortunately so late that we could not have it framed until that day. When he started his speech, there was still no picture on the stage. Then after a few minutes it arrived, the gold bronze of the frame still wet. The others said, it could not be put up at this time. But I said, 'The picture must go up!' Therefore, I grabbed the damp sticky heavy frame, went on stage from the side and placed the picture under the eyes of the 3,000 spectators behind Maharishi. He continued speaking unmoved. I think I did the right thing, even though my smart dark blue suit suffered a bit and I had to clean my hands of gold bronze for ten minutes in the Gent's room.

Then I could finally sit down in the first row, where a seat had been saved for me. And that was the end of my wakefulness. After all, I had practically not slept for several nights. During Maharishi's whole speech I only sometimes heard people laughing, otherwise I did not hear a word or have a thought. Only when Maharishi invited the public to ask questions, I woke up again. A long queue of questioners formed behind the microphone in the parquet. Strangely enough, they were hardly questions about the global cause of the event, but mostly questions from meditators about their meditation.

Although 'only' about 3,000 people had come, the whole event was a great success for me. It turned out later that there were more people attending here than in the larger cities of Hamburg and Berlin, although, e.g., in Hamburg, there was a larger percentage of meditators in the population than in Munich, at times up to a third of the inhabitants! The other cities had apparently not done as preparation much as we had done.

After the lecture, I had to take care of the dismantling of the decoration and the like. Late in that night, I arrived with the truck in front of our Center. When it was finally finished, I should actually have fallen into bed. But I thought, 'I wonder if Maharishi was still receiving people?' I drove to his hotel.

In one of the halls, there was a meeting of the TM teachers and meditators with Mr. Ritterstaedt. When I joined him, he greeted me in front of everyone and praised my work. I shied away; after all, I had spent most of the time travelling around the Centers. I sat down in one of the last rows – this was actually not what I was interested in. Finally, I discreetly left the hall and went to Maharishi's suite.

Indeed, apparently some of our people were still with him, even though it was so late. I too was let in, came into the dimly lit room and sat down in the back row. I don't remember what Maharishi was talking about. Nevertheless, what I do remember is that he repeatedly looked at me with a serious, somewhat worried expression and looked at me longer. He probably saw that I was totally overtired and exhausted. What he was really thinking, I never found out, of course. He did not intervene by giving me personal advice. After all, everyone had to take care of themselves, how else could one really learn?

The next day some of us drove behind Maharishi to the airport from where he was supposed to fly to Hamburg. It was another bright June day. Again, I was able to go with Adolf to the runway. Maharishi was still waiting for a fellow passenger, Princess Blücher. So, he simply stood in front of the small plane in the sun, said nothing and enjoyed the day. We stood in a small circle around him. It was one of those happy moments in life.

After Maharishi had departed, I sat in my car and travelled, quasi behind him, to Hamburg. That means, actually a friend was driving the car, he and his wife were sitting in front and I lay down in the back seat. I do not think I could have driven at all. Only gradually did the over-excitement subside, and I fell asleep.

We arrived just in time for the Hamburg event at the Congress Center. The hall was full, but it was much smaller than ours. During the break, Maharishi accepted flowers; I gave him one too, but he did not pay any attention to me: This was no longer my place and my Center.

After the talk, there was another meeting with the National Director. I sat in one of the back rows. Mr. Ritterstaedt asked me to tell Maharishi something about our success in Munich. I stood up, but could hardly move my lips because of tiredness. I had the feeling that I was babbling more or less, but it probably did not seem so to the others.

After an overnight stay at my mother's house, I went back to Munich and from there to the next ATR course in Courchevel, a winter health resort in the French Alps. The course was again very enjoyable.

As usual, the course participants were spread over many hotels in the town. Maharishi stayed in the Hotel Annapurna, which was located far above the village, and was difficult to reach on foot, especially with us being so delicate from the long meditations. However, since I had my car with me, I took the liberty of driving up there from time to time and sitting down for meetings with Maharishi.

He held his meetings in the hall of the swimming pool there. On the area next to the pool, they had set up some chairs. Because of this setup a very funny thing happened, which was told to me later: Maharishi wanted to inaugurate new TM teachers or give out a special technique or something similar. For this purpose, 'puja tables' had been set up on the relatively narrow sidewalks around the pool: small improvised tables for the puja, which each of the participants had to perform before their 'initiation'. Everyone performed the ceremony at the same time; afterwards, everyone was to go to Maharishi and receive his mantra.[*6] At the end of the ceremony, one normally knelt down in front of the 'altar', with the picture of Guru Dev. One of the participants stepped back a little too far and fell into the water. To the cheers of all the others and to the amusement of Maharishi, he climbed out of the pool in his good suit, dripping, and went to Maharishi to get his instruction.

At the end of the Course, we all received a special advanced technique. During the preparatory session with Maharishi, one very eager participant accused another of passing on confidential teaching information. Maharishi dug deeper and, with a few questions, found that the person making the accusation had virtually lured the information out of the other. Both were subsequently not admitted to the special technique instructions. What impressed me was that I felt Maharishi's wrath shooting down on my neighbor, the zealot sitting right next to me, like a wave of power; and that I got some distinct splashes from it. I actually felt a guilty conscience, perhaps because I was always very concerned not to divulge secret information, and I never did.

At the end of the session, I stood up and asked Maharishi if I could participate in the instruction although I came a little late to this course. The argument, that I had been late because of the Munich event, did not seem to impress him. Then in time, I had the idea to say that I had already participated in six previous ATR courses. Thereupon I got the okay.

Düsseldorf

In 1975, life took me to Düsseldorf, the administrative headquarters of the German TM movement. By 'coincidence' I was there as part of my coordinator job just when it became known that the WDR (main radio station in Germany) wanted to broadcast a fiercely critical report against TM in its 'Monitor' program. We decided, within a few days, to file a 'temporary injunction' against it. Someone had to organize it, and since I was there, the choice fell on me. The temporary injunction was approved by the court, but WDR did not abide by it. Therefore, we decided to file a huge claim for damages. Again, someone had to coordinate this, and again it was me who was chosen. And so, I stayed in Düsseldorf for the time being.

Through this I became, almost unnoticed, an employee of the German TM headquarters. After a miserable failure of the legal process, I was given the position of Director of Expansion, and finally I even became National Director, when the National Leader, Mr. Ritterstaedt, was absent for six months.

Of course, this was again an exhausting time, and so I was glad to be able to participate in an ATR course over Christmas, in Biarritz in the south of France. At the end of this course, we participants drove to Vitznau in Switzerland, where Maharishi wanted to see us. In the old 'Vitznauer Hof' I moved into the most delightful room of my life, directly above the Lake Lucerne.

By relaxing on the Course, I was able to enjoy everything incredibly more deeply. Moreover, I could rely on my intuition so much that I always felt exactly when Maharishi would come. While the others waited in the hall for hours, I rested in my room and read in a book, and only just before Maharishi appeared, did I go inside. At the end of these few days, I had a one-on-one conversation with Maharishi, as did many others.

Afterwards I went back to Norf, near Düsseldorf, where I lived with nine members of the German TM administrative center. In spring, Mr. Ritterstaedt went to Switzerland for a six-month advanced training course, the participating TM teachers were to be trained: 'Governors of the Age of Enlightenment', 'Governors' because, after the course, they were supposed to be able to control the laws of nature by mastering the subtle levels of consciousness. During Ritterstaedt's absence, I automatically grew into the role of his deputy. And now that I was the boss, the whole burden of the Movement lay on my shoulders. Soon I needed urgent recovery, but could not go on any ATR course, since there was no replacement for me.

Once I went to Seelisberg for official reasons. Besides, I wished to ask Maharishi there whether I should go on the next 'Governor's course'. However, year by year it became more and more difficult to get to Maharishi. But, when he once wanted to leave with a helicopter from his small departure point behind the Hotel Sonnenberg, I was lucky: I heard the helicopter coming and hurried up to the departure place. Maharishi was driven by car to the edge of the grass field. On his way to the plane, I tried to approach him, but was pulled back by his secretary Ron by the tail of my jacket. I fought against it and Ron finally released me when he noticed that Maharishi turned towards me in a friendly way. His answer to my question was a very definite 'yes.'

From that moment on, I received support from all corners in the right direction: I found a successor for my job, was able to sell my worn-out car for 500 marks, which enabled me to pay the course fee exactly, using all my saved ATR credit, and found carpooling opportunities, which took me over several stations to the door of the Course hotel. That was the end of my phase in the German headquarters. Totally exhausted from the last six months, practically crawling on my hands and knees, I arrived in Interlaken at the beginning of the course.

Training to be 'Governor of the Age of Enlightenment'

The aim of the six-month Course was, as already mentioned, training to become a 'Governor of the Age of Enlightenment'. In practical terms, this meant learning the 'TM Sidhis', which Maharishi had recently developed as an advanced technique of Transcendental Meditation. Their purpose was to enable the practitioner to produce effects on the outer level of phenomena from the finest level of consciousness, purely through mental impulses in a very quiet state. One of these 'Sidhis' was 'Yogic Flying', which is quite well known to the public today, but was completely new at that time and also unimaginable for us. One day, foam mats were actually delivered, obviously to cushion the landing. This thing called flying seemed to be meant to be taken seriously!

After some preparatory weeks of fasting, the important day came when Maharishi was to attend the Course. In a way, this day became a disaster that many of us would remember for decades to come. Among the participants was a small group of 'top people', – secretaries of Maharishi and other top officials who, secretly admired, set the tone. Shortly before the great day, one of them stood up, it was John B., whom I personally admired especially because of his calm charisma, and presented an idea they had developed in their group. He said that it was written repeatedly in the Holy Scriptures that the disciple had to clearly tell the master that he wanted enlightenment from him. The suggestion was this: when Maharishi came, everyone should chant a portion of the puja in front of him, bow to the ground, and then someone should present the collective request of all participants to attain enlightenment at this class.

It is important to know that the puja contains a traditional praise of the spiritual teacher, in our case Guru Dev. Chanting the puja in front of Maharishi would have lifted him to the level of his own Master, something Maharishi had always strictly avoided. He had never called himself a Master at all and had always placed himself far below his teacher. A discussion arose among the participants of the Course: A few did not feel quite comfortable with the matter, but most agreed, especially since the suggestion came from the top group who were expected to know Maharishi better.

When the day arrived, Maharishi climbed up onto the stage, which was particularly high this time (for practical reasons, tables were used as a base, not the usual crates). Now came one of the most embarrassing moments of my life: Everyone sang the puja or a part of it together and bowed deeply to the floor. Then one of the leaders in the group stood up, I would not have liked to be in his shoes, and read a text at the end of which, after some praise, it said, 'We ask for enlightenment on this Course.'

It was all so artificial and childish that I would have loved to sink into the ground. I had not expected that before. I could not even look at Maharishi properly to see how he reacted. It was horrible. After a relatively short speech, Maharishi left the hall without reacting to the ceremony. The next day we received our instructions as if nothing had happened.

At our next meeting, one of the instructors remarked that he had seen how complacently Maharishi had reacted. In fact, the opposite was true: Maharishi told to some people that he suddenly felt completely alien to us and distant. More than that, he believed that the initiators were working for the CIA and wanted to discredit our Movement by trying to put him on the pedestal of a religious Master.

He came briefly to see us a few more times to give us further instructions for the Sidhis. Even the group of top people were able to finish their Course, but after that, they were all not allowed to attend any international Course for many years, even decades. This seemed to me personally to be extremely harsh. What was the reason behind Maharishi's strong reaction? I could not imagine John, in particular, had any devious intentions. Somehow, it must have been good for the course participants.

When John was not allowed to attend Courses for years, I decided to intercede for him with Maharishi; unfortunately, this was only after I was no longer secretary and therefore had to wait a long time for an opportunity. Interestingly, Nature did indeed send me such an opportunity, but not until the end of 1994, 18 years after the unfortunate event. At that time, I had been sent to America as a member of Purusha for a special project. There, in teams of one German and three Americans each held presentations in their assigned city, and taught TM to business people… When I arrived in 'my' city of Palo Alto, I learned that John B. was the director of the local TM Center that we Purushas were to work with him. Just at the time of my visit, John received word from the national headquarters that he could not officially be the Director of the Center, although he did an excellent job and was and had remained the soul of the Center. All because of the story of 18 years ago! Therefore, I realized that John was still humiliated.

I introduced myself to John as one of his successors in the secretarial job. We liked each other immediately, and I noticed in our conversations that John was still completely devoted to Maharishi. How else could he have continued to work diligently for the movement for 18 years?

When I returned to Vlodrop in Holland, then the home of the Purusha Group, also where Maharishi resided, one day there was a meeting of all returning Americans. Maharishi wanted to hear the reports about the different cities and activities. I immediately thought, 'This is a chance to mention John.' When it was my turn to speak, after four sentences I was on the topic of John. After the meeting someone told me that another friend of John's had mentioned him to Maharishi less than a year ago, but that time he had reacted very disparagingly. However, this time he was interested and friendly. Nandkishore, the top secretary sitting next to him, reminded Maharishi that John was on the 'black list'. Maharishi asked me, 'Why?', as if he couldn't remember. I briefly told the story, telling how devoted John was in spite of everything, and that he had been actively working for the Movement all along. Maharishi listened to everything and finally said, 'Well, put him back on the White list.' To fill the measure of my joy and pride, he gave me, who at that time had long since ceased to hold a special position, the task of officially announcing John's rehabilitation to the American national leader.

Of course, I then called John myself. We were both deeply touched. The heavy burden of 18 years of exile and humiliation had finally fallen off John. For months on end, I received grateful congratulations from many sides for checking John 'back in' again. Obviously, many had thought the same way I did. By the way, Maharishi stopped the session after my report. I suspected that he had called the whole meeting only to clarify John's situation, because he of course sensed exactly what was going on.

In spite of its unsuccessful start, the Interlaken course went to Maharishi's satisfaction, because he proudly talked about the 200 male TM teachers at the Victoria-Jungfrau Hotel several times afterwards.

I myself was not exactly in bliss during these months, because I did not like the long meditations so much. I was more a person of activity. But, despite my inner restlessness I had some quite interesting spiritual experiences. At that time, Maharishi often spoke of 'ritam', the most subtle level of consciousness one could reach in very deep meditation. He explained that any thought or wish one had at that level would manifest immediately, at least through a clear inner experience.

I had such 'ritam' experiences once or twice. One of them was that I was still dominated by my eating addiction, my 'table tendency', which had been intensified by the long 'rounds' of meditation. For weeks, I desperately longed for a plum cake with cream. Then, one day, during a very quiet meditation, it suddenly appeared before my inner eye: a wonderful plum cake, with cream and everything that went with it, as clear as an advertising photo. Not only did I see this cake, no, I smelled and tasted it with the same intensity. If a material plum cake had been standing in front of me, I would not have experienced it so clearly and intensively. Therefore, that was the fulfilment of my wish: All senses were satisfied. I was completely satisfied by this experience, which was in no way inferior to a 'real' experience: After all, every external experience is a state of consciousness anyway, and this one was even better than if I had eaten this delicacy in a café. After this meditation experience my longing for plum cake was gone – the desire had been fulfilled on a deep level.

Another time it was with yoghurt: I saw very clearly, closely and vividly how yoghurt flowed out of a drinking glass. Then I looked into the glass, which was suddenly empty and clean. While standing in line for lunch, when I grabbed my dishes, I took a drinking glass from the shelf, lost in thought. I somehow suspected that it might not be completely clean, held it up against the light closely and looked down at its inside bottom. Suddenly I realized that this was exactly the same image, the same close view of a drinking glass bottom, as in the morning in meditation. So, this had not only been a 'ritam' experience, but also a small precognition. 'Not bad,' I thought.

A few weeks after the beginning of the Course we finally received the instruction into the 'Sidhis' and finally also in the 'Yogic Flying'. As I said, the mats had already been laid out, and from the previous six-month Course, those who had extended and attended a continuation Course came to us to 'fly in'; to serve as a model, so to speak.

When in this first flight session the bell signal sounded – as a signal to now begin with the 'Flying Sutra'[15] (a small formula to be thought of inwardly), we beginners naturally blinked in order to see what was happening with the advanced students. That was an exciting moment. At first, nothing happened, but then some of the old ones started to shake, then jerked up and down a bit and finally, in lotus position, hopped like a frog. Many of us burst out laughing; it looked so funny. However, we also saw that the 'flyers' were completely relaxed and having a lot of fun themselves. They were beaming with joy. The 'take-off' was obviously effortless and happened all by itself, just by this inner impulse. Inspired by the advanced flyers, after a few minutes a few new ones started to hop up and down, mostly still quite awkwardly, and partly without having mastered the lotus position.

In the following days, the whole atmosphere vibrated with the joyful excitement of those who had flying experiences themselves and with the unrestrained desire of the others also to have such seemingly extremely satisfying experiences. Nothing happened for a few days in my case. I sat as heavy as a stone on the mat and envied those who were already taking off. I desperately, wanted to fly, but effort was of no avail, on the contrary, it had to come by itself, without effort.

One evening I watched how it started with Dr. Bernd Zeiger, who I knew well. Bernd was actually a rather sober type, a scientist, certainly not a 'mood-maker'. He had been sitting loosely cross-legged; he was too stiff for the right lotus position. Now he was suddenly pulled upwards, his legs unfolding. Immediately he fell back onto the mat; but no sooner had he touched the floor than it pulled him up again, and so it went on: sometimes diagonally to the upper right, then to the left again; his arms and legs waved wildly around the room. Bernd yelled and laughed and cheered. He was obviously completely at the mercy of the impulses.

This impressed me so much that my longing to fly too became almost unbearable. I remember that I could hardly sleep that night; everything in me vibrated with excited energy. The next morning, we sat on the mat again: first meditation, then the Sidhi Sutras, and then the Flying Sutra was to come. I was already waiting inwardly for the bell signal when we were all still busy with the preceding sutras.

These related to the mastery of the five elements, including the mastery of the air. Suddenly I noticed how I began to breathe heavily, and then more and more heavily and violently. I was panting in rhythm like a walrus. Then it happened: with each violent inhalation, my body lifted up and with each exhalation sank back to the rolled-up blanket I was sitting on. From inhalation to inhalation I became lighter and lighter. Then suddenly I had no more weight; I was actually light as air! I still thought, 'Actually it is still too early, the Flying Sutra has not yet begun.' But then, I let myself go. I had the idea, 'Now I have to jump properly.' However, it did not work. It lifted me up in the air so that my legs unfolded and I came up with elbows and knees; and then it pushed me over the mats, which were still completely empty at the time.

I was propelled like an air-inflated balloon, blown over the ground by the wind, touching the ground only here and there. My knees and elbows touched the ground every few meters, but then I flew straight back in the air, completely unorthodox and without style. By the time the bell signal sounded for the start of 'flying', it was over for me. I tried to think the Flying Sutra in order to 'fly' correctly, as it was intended. But nothing moved anymore. I just stayed between the people hopping around me, with my body vibrating with happiness, still full of lightness, and at the same time with the pride of having 'taken off' now, and not badly so. Afterwards others congratulated me and commented on my unusual show.

I remained for hours with a feeling of happiness, lightness and freedom. Nevertheless, I was not completely satisfied, as I had not created the effect by conscious thinking of the Sutra; on the contrary, when I had tried it, nothing more had happened. The thing was that the extremely intense desire had seeped into such a deep layer of consciousness that it had unfolded its effect there and produced the lightness. By the way, this probably was not the lightness of Akasha (space) that was intended, but the lightness of air, the mastery of which had been the subject of the previous sutra. I had not been absolutely weightless, but, according to the theory of the Yoga Sutras, my body had been transformed into the quality of the element air, not so bad anyway!

At the next session the heavy breathing started again, unfortunately also again 'too early'. Again, I became lighter and lighter with every breath. But then, I held myself back a little bit and thought, 'Hold it back a little more until the time for the Flying Sutra. Otherwise people will think I'm not doing the Flying Sutra!' Unfortunately, the effort of having these thoughts stifled the spontaneous event. When the little bell sounded and I took up the Flying Sutra, nothing more happened. I remained seated. What a pity! In addition, in the next days and weeks I could not get myself up anymore. Apparently, I had tensed up too much, so that I could not reach the necessary subtle level of consciousness.

I got back into flying only through a trick that I had learned: I simply began to hop forward cross-legged, consciously and willingly, during the flight program. After a few landings, I noticed that suddenly lightness appeared and an energy at the end of the spine drove me up to another hop. Later, it was enough if I simply sat down with the desire to fly, and the automatic impulse to hop came, which took me into the air. However, I never experienced the absolute weightlessness of the first day again. Nevertheless, every flying program brought me energy, lightness, liveliness and joy in all the following years. Really an amazing technique Maharishi had developed! Therefore, these were my most important experiences during this Course. Apart from that, I was a little bored and was quite satisfied as the end approached.

After the Course, we learned what Maharishi intended to do with us new 'Governors of the Age of Enlightenment'. We were to organize and hold Courses in our own countries, each in teams of four, to prepare meditators for learning the 'Sidhis' through weeklong preparatory courses of 'rounding' and deepening of knowledge. All course participants were excited about these new perspectives. Except myself. I had no desire to return 'to the field'. What was there to gain from it? In principle, I thought I had already gone through everything. It became routine again and again. I wanted to stay with Maharishi.

Seelisberg – the International Headquarters

On one of the last days of the Course, it was now May 1977; we were all in Seelisberg in the Hotel Sonnenberg. We sat in the large hall with its semicircular rows of chairs, each of which, rising slightly like in an amphitheater, was separated by a continuous wide, upholstered row of tables. Maharishi was not personally present, but was connected to us by video. We saw him on the screens, and he saw us, who were being targeted by various cameras.

This meeting dealt with the consolidation of the teams of four: Who is working with whom? Which team goes to which city or cities? Almost all of them could hardly wait to get into this project. Maharishi truly understood how to motivate people. Soon, all teams of four were sitting together.

Only two people stayed behind, Wolfgang Döring, whom I had met on the Course, and me. We did not want to go out 'into the field', but to work here on the 'International Staff'. That seemed almost absurd in this situation, as it was obvious what Maharishi expected from us.

Finally, Maharishi asked, 'Is there anyone else left?' Wolfgang and I stood up. The camera panned over and zoomed in on us. Wolfgang expressed his wish. After some hesitation, Maharishi said, 'Yes, you can stay.'

Then he asked, 'And the other one?' I explained that I wanted to stay in Seelisberg and work in the video department, in what is known as 'video duplication', i. e. the duplication of video tapes that were then sent to the Centers and Academies. I had already looked into the video department during one of my visits as a representative of our national headquarters. In the 'Duplication Corner', 20 to 30 video recorders were humming next to and below each other. At that time, we still had the large U-matic video machines. Above each column of recorders a monitor showed what was being duplicated,-of course always some lecture by Maharishi. That gave, despite all the technology, a very homey feeling.

That is where I wanted to go: all day long, this stimulating humming of the machines, and in doing so, besides the work, automatically draw in Maharishi's knowledge. Moreover, after the stress of my previous work, I wanted a simple job with not too much responsibility: Just insert tapes, turn on the machines, make sure everything is running, and wait until I could take the tapes out of the machines. I imagined that to be nice and comfortable.

After I had presented my request, Maharishi asked, 'What did you do so far?' I tried to be modest: Center manager, regional coordinator, most recently work in the German headquarters. Maharishi just sat there and kept quiet. For several minutes, nothing could be heard and he did not make a sound. I felt quite uneasy and I thought, 'Failure! Maybe he has something against me.'

Finally, after anxious minutes, he said like casually and uninterested, 'You can stay.' Whew! Deep breath on my side. 'But use your talents. Sit down with Vesey (the top secretary at the time) and Peter (who was in charge of the video department and everything electrical at the time) and find a job.'

Only later did I learn more or less what had happened. Maharishi had been sitting in a 'meeting room' in his suite; around him were many close associates, including the man responsible for the video. He had turned the sound off from time to time when one of the people in this room made a remark or a comment. Obviously, some people had now stood up for me, among them probably Vesey, who knew me as the head of the German headquarters, and Peter P., who knew of me as a successful TM teacher. Therefore, it happened that Maharishi, who already knew me, wanted to give me a more responsible job than just putting in tapes. So, I was accepted into the international staff.

This was going to be a new, completely different challenge. I got a small room in the Hotel Kulm. Maharishi himself had his suite on the third floor of the Kulm and always went over to the Sonnenberg for the more public meetings. He took the elevator down to the first floor, walked down the corridor to the end of the building, where the small covered and enclosed bridge led across the street to the Sonnenberg. This was one of the ways to approach Maharishi and ask him something. At that time, he was still encouraging people to do so. In this way he could even while walking, keep projects going that needed his decisions and solve small questions and problems.

Right on the first day Peter assigned me my job. I was to become the coordinator, practically a leader, of the entire video department, whose sub-departments had worked more or less side by side until then. There were the areas 'audio editing', 'audio duplication', 'video editing', 'video duplication', 'titling' and 'video library'. The 'official language' was English, of course.

Unfortunately, I didn't have the slightest idea about electronics, as I had only worked as a philosopher and teacher before. Now I was even supposed to run the department! As I later found out, this was typical for Maharishi. He preferred to put people into projects they did not understand. Ultimately, he was more concerned with his students developing through the difficulties than through their performance being excellent from the outset.

The video department was located in a large room that might have served as a dining hall in the past. Its panoramic windows gave a fantastic view of the lake and the mountains. Countless machines hummed, the monitors flickered; there was a tangle of cables everywhere. The whole thing was so confusing and unknown to me that, contrary to Maharishi's actual idea, I hid in the duplication department at first.

There I learned the necessary steps and became somewhat more familiar with the master-machines, on which the large rolls of 'Edited Master' were played and transferred to the many video-cassette recorders. After a short time, I moved this subdivision to a neighboring room, because everything in the main room was packed so tightly that people were stepping on each other's toes. However, I first had to create the new room by partitioning off a kind of foyer with large chipboard planks – for which I had to work my way through the administrative and financial apparatus of the head office until I got the new room, the planks and the work approved. After a few weeks, Maharishi came to our department. He did not like the dark brown wall he had to walk past because it took the light away from the foyer. Therefore, we had to dismantle the wall the next day, which was great fun, by the way.

The subdivision had to go back to where it came from, but it was placed a bit better and more orderly. During his visit, Maharishi did not pay any attention to 'my' duplication department at all, but went directly to the main room where the 'editing' took place – in film business one would probably speak of 'cutting'. Maharishi was interested in the new Ampex master machines, of which quite a few had just been purchased.

I rushed in behind him, and I was almost embarrassed that I now had to explain to him the workings of these machines, which had just been bought and which I only had barely gotten to know. Maharishi, however, was satisfied with my explanations. After this meeting, it was clear to me that I needed to become more familiar with the editing department, and so I did. However, I kept a somewhat uneasy feeling almost until the end of my time in 'video', because I had never worked on the cutting machines myself. It took quite a long time before I even got an idea of what to do in editing. My usual strategy of first reading a book about the whole area helped me a little, but it was not enough.

I had been imposed on the department from outside and never had the time to learn the technical details. Soon waves of organizational work were crashing down on me. We got the instructions about which Courses to edit from which lectures of Maharishi. I realized that my task was to keep the machines running. I had to provide the video technicians with the original masters they needed, often several at the same time. I had to make sure that fresh blank rolls of tape were always available, that the machines worked, coordinate the use of the machine sets, and give the editors the transcripts and explain them if necessary.

We received these transcripts from the 'Ladies', but we never got to see them in person, because in the whole headquarters – which at that time, I think, was already called 'Capital of the Age of Enlightenment', or 'Capital' for short – women and men lived strictly separated. At the times when everyone met in the general assembly hall, women sat on the right and the men on the left. These 'Ladies' were veteran TM teachers whom Maharishi had trained to decide which sections of his lectures to use for Courses, which to cut out, which to add from other recordings, and so on. My job required my full attention. There were so many little details to think about. One day, still in the early days, I had the idea of painting a large chart of the video department's entire work, with all the subdivisions and all the jobs in progress, to keep Maharishi informed of the progress of the work.

Therefore, I sat down with my roll of paper in the 'Gold Room' – so called because the carpet, all wallpaper, all chairs and their covers were in gold or golden yellow. There Maharishi met with some staff members almost every day. Sitting in one of the back rows, I waited for an opportunity to speak. This opportunity came. I got up and held up my display board. I knew that Maharishi's attention would usually be immediately attracted when someone held up such a chart, because he loved these charts.

I started my explanations, but things soon turned out differently than I had hoped. Maharishi was very unhappy with the speed of our production. I stood there flushed all over and endured his scolding. Maharishi demanded that we work in shifts around the clock to increase production. Downcast, I immediately ran into our department, called the people together and told them about Maharishi's dissatisfaction. Secretly I was happy to have a means in my hand to spur my boys to more productivity. I divided them into shifts.

From then on, the machines were humming day and night for many months. I had to whiz around 24 hours a day to see that everything was running, that all had their materials, so they could work.

By accident, and appropriately, I was assigned a room directly above the video department so that I could constantly hear the sound of the machines. I could tell when things were a little quieter. Then I knew that not all the machines were working, so I raced down to check. The floor of my room was in such a bad condition that I could even look through a hole between the planks into the video room if I took the thin carpet aside.

The constant pressure was enormous and sometimes brought me to the edge of my nervous power. Especially when there were additional 'rush jobs', when special tapes had to be produced very quickly for some conference or course that was to start in a few days, then several shifts worked in parallel until they fell over. However, not with a hidden grumble, quite the opposite: these were always the best days. We were vibrating with excitement and enthusiasm because we were obviously part of very important projects that would change the world. Totally exhausted, we sat after such project in the dining room together and were simply happy.

In general, the whole 'Capital' lived from rush jobs, some department always had one. Maharishi developed a tremendous creativity in inventing projects that were very urgent and extremely important. So, we always had the feeling of being at the center of the world. What an exciting and happy time it was for all of us! There was always something special going on. Conferences at the 'Capital', big conferences elsewhere for which we had to prepare something quickly.

Moreover, if there were no rush jobs, there were other excitements: Is Maharishi coming to the Great Hall today? Is he in the Gold Room right now? Who is he meeting there? Maybe I can sit and listen after work? Will the WYMS let me in?

Another diversion usually happened just before the full moon. Then there were, at least in summer, 'boat rides' on the lake. Everybody was allowed to join. Mostly, of course at the last minute, because Maharishi always decided spontaneously, three pleasure boats were rented; we already knew them. One ship was reserved for Maharishi, for his most important people and, of course, invited guests. The other two ships were for the lower grades.

Of course, for those who had already worked their way up, there was always the exciting question: Who is allowed on Maharishi's boat today? He decided each time anew. The secretaries presented him with a list, which he approved or modified according to his feelings. In the evening then, rows of cars would be on the winding road, bridging 400m difference in altitude, down to the lake. The boats were already there. In front of Maharishi's boat, stood the WYMS security people, letting only the invited ones on board. Maharishi always came at the very end with the secretary on duty and perhaps one or two very important guests. In the middle of the lake, the ships were often tied together and cables were laid across the water between the boats so that what was being said on the main boat could be heard through speakers in the other ships. Most of the time, however, this only worked imperfectly. At least on the side ships we got a whiff of the relaxed and easygoing conversations Maharishi had with his guests.

A particularly wild full moon trip is still in my memory. As soon as we left the moorings, Maharishi's ship darted off, so that the other two had difficulty to keep up. I stood on the deck of the second fastest ship and could see Maharishi's boat rushing forward in the bright moonlight, quite far in the distance. It went to Altdorf at the southern end of the lake. There the ship entered the small harbor. We curved around outside the harbor and waited. The captain had no idea what was going on. Finally, we persuaded him to enter the harbor as well. Just as we were approaching the harbor entrance, Maharishi's ship pushed out again. However, it didn't set off, but made a big circle in front of the harbor. We always followed. The third ship was nowhere to be seen. It had lost us. Then the main ship drove back into port. Just as we were about to follow after some time, it came out and made big turns again. And so, it went on. We were constantly focused on Maharishi and his ship, and felt more and more confused.

Finally, the main ship rushed back home after a few rounds and that was it. Afterwards we learned that Maharishi had had the idea to have ice cream brought from a café in Altdorf for the guests. That is why they had moored there, and one of them had started with the task to organize the ice cream. When he was not back after some time, Maharishi let the ship run out of the harbor and circled around outside. Then it went back to the dock. The boy was still not back. So, it went out again. And that happened several times. During the time, Maharishi talked animatedly with the guests until finally the ice cream had been brought to the quay.

Another diversion that always brought excitement to the Capital were the conferences to which top scientists from outside were invited. Maharishi always placed great emphasis on ensuring that Transcendental Meditation and all his teachings were recognized by established science. In this way he wanted to gradually integrate TM into the educational system. He obviously hoped that if all schools and universities had meditators and taught SCI, the Science of Creative Intelligence, we would truly enter the Age of Enlightenment. Again, and again he had conferences on specific topics organized in our Capital, for example on quantum theory, on the basics of biology and other topics. At that time, we were sometimes visited by very distinguished scientists such as the Nobel Prize winner for physics, Brian Josephson and other well-known physicists, biologists, chemists and literary scientists. The conferences were moderated by our own PhD scientists. These were mostly long-time followers of Maharishi, who lived at Capital and were well educated.

During these conferences, we were allowed to leave our work and play a competent audience. We enjoyed the variety and the lively atmosphere of these days. The sessions were usually held in such a way that the guests gave their lectures and Maharishi gave his comments either in between or after. The details that the speaker wanted to convey were ignored; Maharishi always presented his own philosophy and message very quickly. I was sometimes surprised that people accepted it so peacefully. They always listened attentively, and, being creative and big thinking, as most were, they got something out of it.

Once there was a conference called 'Law, Justice and Rehabilitation'. A rather boring subject, it seemed to me. The main speaker was one of the highest judges (or even the highest judge) of the Supreme Court of India, Justice Iyer, a quite brilliant speaker. At one of the sessions the man at the video mixer failed completely by accidentally not plugging in our modern and professional Marconi cameras, but instead an old small secondary camera, which was actually only supposed to record marginal scenes. By chance, I was operating this very camera – the first and only time I tried my hand at being a cameraman, and didn't do a very good job of it. The camera did not have a monitor yet. I had to look through an eyepiece, which was very strenuous for the eyes. Because of the bad tripod, the picture kept slipping away from me. But exactly these pictures were all we had on tape from this meeting. The people at the editing machines then tried to make the best out of it with 'cover shots'.

Soon after, another group of important guests arrived, and one afternoon when Maharishi had something else to do, he ordered these people to listen to the above law-conference on video. And there I made a big mistake that could easily have cost me my job. Nevertheless, fortunately, the two secretaries, Vesey and Neil, turned a blind eye since I was so new and had shown overall good will. The tapes of this conference had not yet been duplicated. Therefore, you could only play them directly from the master reel. The big master machines were located in the video room at the Kulm. However, the guests were supposed to watch the conference in a hall in the Sonnenberg. Therefore, a long cable was laid through the corridors and across the bridge. The tapes were to be played on my master-machine, with which I otherwise had to duplicate the normal tapes for the field. My extra job for the guests, playing the law-conference tapes, went for many, many hours, so I was not able to do my normal job of duplicating other tapes. I must admit I did not like the conference. I found it boring, and simply could not imagine that anyone could be interested in it. Therefore, after a while I simply unplugged the cable that led into the hall. A few hours later, Maharishi found out that the guests were sitting around idly. Of course, he was quite angry then, especially since he was apparently infatuated with this conference. The secretaries came and upbraided and scolded me – and rightly so. I stood there red-faced and could only weakly talk my way out, that I had the order to duplicate other tapes. The secretaries appreciated that I was still a beginner in dealing with Maharishi. I still had to learn that the wishes of the master always had top priority. It was on this principle that our entire Vedic system of enlightenment was ultimately based: that one's thinking was completely attuned to the Master.

Overall, however, I felt that Maharishi was probably satisfied with me. I estimate that during my time in the video department the total production increased tenfold. This was partly because we had just gotten the new Ampex machines, which had many quirks but were much easier to operate, compared to the old and cumbersome IVC colossuses. However, it was also due to my dedication and coordination. One aspect of my work was that I had to keep the machines running at all times. And indeed, they often failed, because they had just been newly developed and contained many unproven technologies. Actually, we would have needed a specialist electronics engineer, preferably one from the company Ampex itself, unfortunately, we only had one engineer, Peter P., the same one who got me into this job. He hardly ever had time to help and was hardly ever to be seen in the video room because he had other tasks. My main technician was Johannes Seefluth, who was more or less just a tinkerer. He never had any specialist training, but he had a knack for fixing things. The secret of his success was that he loved the machines. Whenever a machine went on strike, as I observed, it was very often due to the fact that the machine operator was under stress, under pressure, distracted or whatever, and his tension disturbed the sensitive electronics. I then called Johannes; he arrived quite calmly, often too slowly –in my opinion, but this calmness was the secret of his success. He usually switched the machine off at first. Then he stroked it several times and switched it on again. And, you would not believe it, in most cases it ran again. During this time, I learned that also machines are like living beings, which have their moods and which react to the very 'sensitive' to the state of mind of their users. In the end, like all beings, they rejoice in love, and Johannes could give them that more than anyone else could.

And what came out of all our efforts? Row after row of 'Edited Masters'. Most of them for the extensive 'Invincibility Course', in which Maharishi wanted to put all his knowledge, at least as much as he thought was digestible. He had recorded hundreds of hours especially for this series of tapes. Ten years later, I heard from the Tape Librarian that this Course had never been used – at least not in the planned complete version. So, what was our work good for? I am inclined to think that it was mainly for us, that is, for those who had worked on it. We had evolved through it.

I am moving up: Organization of the 'Sidhi Center Course'

After about a year and a half, I began to feel a certain dissatisfaction with the job. Although there were countless changes and challenges, I gradually became familiar with the principle of the whole thing. Moreover, if there is one thing I cannot stand, it's routine. So, one day I decided to ask Maharishi for another job. I stood in front of the Gold Room where Maharishi was holding a 'meeting', in order to accost him. As he stepped out, I stepped up to him and talked to him as he crossed the bridge over to the Kulm. I told him that I wanted to do something else. He asked me, 'What do you want to do?' I honestly told him, 'I don't know. I only know that I want to stay with you.'

That sounded, it seemed to me at the time, probably a bit pompous and pathetic. But later I realized that my answer had been decisive. For there seems to be a cosmic law: What you want must be clearly stated. Perhaps there was another principle that was specific to the relationship with the Master. Later, when I was Maharishi's secretary, there were two situations when someone came to me and said he would like to be Maharishi's secretary, the highest dream of all. In both cases, I felt that I had to tell Maharishi, no matter how small the chances were. In both cases, he reacted surprisingly attentively and positively, and wanted to see the person personally.

After my answer on the Kulm Bridge, he did not react further. Someone else came up and asked a question. The next morning, at 8 o' clock in the morning, I was still sleeping. Peter S., then his secretary, came into my room with a telephone and said, 'Maharishi wants to talk to you'. There was total excitement on my side; this had never happened before. Peter dialed Maharishi's secret number, said, 'Hans is here,' gave me the machine and disappeared.

What followed was the longest personal conversation I have ever had with Maharishi; it lasted over an hour. Maharishi asked me about my studies, was impressed that I had received my doctorate from Weizsäcker, and said I should contact him and inform him about TM.

At the end of the conversation, he asked again what I wanted to do. I repeated yesterday's answer. He asked, 'What was the direction of your thinking?' I said, 'Maybe MERU[*16] Faculty', that is, to be a faculty member at our private Maharishi European Research University; that would have meant to be a lecturer. Maharishi said 'Hmm', as much as: not a bad idea.

Then I said, 'Another idea was, Veda Group.' This was a recently established small group which was studying Vedic literature and, among other things, was making overview tables of the structure of the Veda. Again, he made 'Hmm'.

And then, I started stuttering: 'Yes, well, someday... I am not good enough... but someday I would like to be your secretary.' Now it was out. I thought: 'Now he'll finish me off or even send me straight home.' But again, he just said 'Hmm', as if nothing had happened.

We talked for a while, and finally he said, 'So, you will be MERU faculty.' So, this meant 'Lecturer for philosophy in the faculty of the university'. That was a good position, and I felt honored; but in the background, I felt a bit uneasy, because now I had to get back into philosophy, all that intellectual stuff that I thought I had left behind since my doctorate. I immediately felt a certain tension and strain in my head. But, I was quite happy. In a childish way, I told Maharishi that I would send for my books now, but he did not react.

After the phone call, I meditated and wanted to go to the basement for Yogic Flying, where special rooms with mattresses were arranged. Unwashed and only provisionally dressed, I went to the video department to check up on it. There a shift had worked all night as usual. I talked to my people and gave orders. At that moment, someone rushed in and told me to come to the gold room immediately, Maharishi wanted to talk to me. I was a little embarrassed that I had not washed yet and was not dressed properly, but I could not hesitate, that was clear.

In the Gold Room, Maharishi was sitting on his sofa; besides him, only Mister Ritterstaedt was in the room. Opposite Maharishi hung a map of Germany. When I came in, he looked at me only briefly and asked, 'Where are the border crossings to the DDR?' Of course, I had no idea what it was about. Nevertheless, fortunately, I knew quite a lot about German geography and pointed to the right places on the map.

'Good, put little stickers on there.' I had them ready and I stuck them on. Afterwards he talked about the biggest German cities and the location of each TM-Center. Everywhere I had to apply different colored 'stickers' and colored needles, so that the map finally looked like a general staff plan, covered with colored spikes and dots.

I did not ask what it was all about, since I had learned by now that Maharishi did not like it at all when people understood his plans. He was something of a commander and strategist and was always careful to keep 'the other side', which definitely existed, in the dark. At some point, it dawned on me that it was about organizing a 'Sidhi Center Course'. The Sidhis, which up to now had only been taught on international courses, on six-month courses, as I had one behind me, should now be taught in all German centers. Finally, the session ended and Maharishi left the room.

This was the first of many days over the next two or three years when I would not be able to perform a proper 'program', even though this had always been our top priority. It wasn't until a year or two later that I learned that in Maharishi's eyes, meditation and the whole 'program' was pretty unimportant when you were working directly for him. This was in line with the basic principle of the Vedic tradition: the actual development and evolution comes through service to the Master. Maharishi himself had not been able to meditate when he was with his Master, although before he had been practicing meditation gladly and for a long time.

Did I ever mention that in my first Seelisberg year I always had the feeling that Maharishi did not like me? He was always very distant, almost dismissive towards me, at least that is how I felt. I thought, 'Somehow, I must have had bad karma in a past life. Had I betrayed him once?' For a long time, I felt like I did not belong in his environment.

But then, in the spring of 1978, there was a situation in which it seemed as if something was changing. On the ground floor of the Hotel Sonnenberg, a room that had previously served only as a warehouse, was to become the 'Veda Room', a particularly dignified little meeting room with expensive silk wallpaper, stage, large Guru Dev image, golden armchairs, and bookcases for the Vedic scriptures. For several days, Maharishi himself sat on an armchair in the middle of this room and instructed the helpers how to furnish the room. I had some free time and took the chance to be close to Maharishi, lugging chairs, boxes, flower arrangements. Meanwhile, he was talking to some 'Ladies' and administrators sitting around him about upcoming projects. Occasionally he turned briefly to the working helpers and gave new instructions.

He had unimaginable 'brain power' in this respect. He could oversee many, many tasks at once. Wherever he turned his attention, he was immediately aware of the whole situation, gave brief instructions on what the respective helpers had to work on for a longer period of time, while he could concentrate on other things. Most of the time he organized three to five things simultaneously.

During the work in the new Veda room, he gave me some attention. I could see how he appreciated the fact that I wanted to serve him with such zeal. Every time he looked at me or even gave me an order, a feeling of happiness poured through me. I really got going and thought I could 'turn the corner' now with him. A similar feeling of happiness flowed through me when Maharishi mentioned my name for the first time: There must have been several hundred people, the whole staff, in the hall. Maharishi wanted to hear our ideas on how we could create income for the Capital and the Movement. For example, should we start any productions and build companies? I got up and said that our strength is knowledge; we should teach and give courses and nothing else. At some point during the meeting, he referred to my input and said, 'Maybe we should just give courses, like Hans said. I was almost surprised that he knew my name, and was quite embarrassed that he took up my modest and actually self-evident suggestion.

In fact, we later built up companies and bought large farms all over the world in order to practice agriculture, the so-called 'Sidha Lands'. Here the respective workers were to be introduced to meditation and the Sidhis, which would hopefully make them work much more effectively and efficiently. Furthermore, these groups would then create coherence in the whole environment through practicing their 'program'.

Later, there were hundreds of such 'Sidha Lands' on the different continents. I think that these indeed created coherence, and so these enterprises certainly had their purpose. The moneymaking part, however, which Maharishi had originally given as a motive, never worked. Meditation only made the workers more relaxed. All the 'Sidha-Lands' eventually turned out to be financial flops. Tens of millions of dollars were lost. Viewed from the outside, it was a disaster.

Nevertheless, I never doubted for a moment that Maharishi had known from the beginning that financially nothing would come of it. Later on,

I realized far too often, how he was incredibly clever even in practical matters. He always knew in advance exactly how things would develop. For example, years later, when several experts expected incredible profits from a patent that could be bought cheaply, he told me privately after the meeting, 'It's all a mirage.' And, he was right, as usual. For me, however, this meeting, where the idea of 'Sidha Lands' was considered for the first time and he had mentioned my name, had been a milestone.

Now, after my long telephone conversation, his recognition and attention were even more manifest. In the afternoon of the same day Maharishi visited 'my' video department and had us explain the structure of the work and the progress. Then they also spoke about a successor for me. Overall, he was obviously satisfied, but without praising me in any way.

In the days after that, I was more and more involved in the organization of the new 'City Center Course'. A position on MERU Faculty was never mentioned again. In connection with the work for the new course, I was soon even allowed to work in Maharishi's personal suite. This suite, on the third floor of the 'Kulm', consisted of two areas: The inner area was Maharishi's personal room, the outer one contained a meeting room for private meetings and the secretaries' office. The whole complex was on lockdown. Outside the door, the WYMS members were guarding day and night.

The privilege that I now enjoyed was that I was allowed, together with Heiner R., to make phone calls in the small meeting room. There were several telephones for which one did not have to ask the reception for an outside line every time. All day long Heiner and I sat here and called the Centers and the Governors in Germany to set up a team of four in every major city to lead the Courses. Heiner was responsible for northern Germany, I was in charge of the south. The whole of Germany lay before us like a chessboard, on which we moved the Governors back and forth like pawns and bishops. Of course, any TM teacher who was not tied to one place by job or family was ready for Maharishi to go wherever he was needed. Still, there was a lot of back and forth until all the teams were finalized.

Every now and then Maharishi would walk through our workroom; it was, after all, the passageway to his private rooms. As was the custom according to Vedic principles, we jumped up and placed hands together in greeting, often a little awkward when we still had the phone in our hands. Maharishi would then usually stop, smile, and inquire about the progress of the project. This was obviously very important to him. Those who were on the other end of the line sometimes told us afterwards that a shiver ran down their spines when they heard Maharishi's voice in the background so unexpectedly. And, we felt naturally great with that.

Once Maharishi tested my effectiveness, which of course I did not suspect at the time. He was having a meeting in the Gold Room, and I was there for some reason. Since there was no secretary at hand, he asked me to connect him with the national director of Venezuela. I still remember his name, which I had never heard before: Villanueva.

I went outside the door, where there were telephones connected to the telephone sets on Maharishi's table in the Gold Room, and thought, 'No problem; Eileen from the communications department will surely know the number.' But it wasn't like that. I called all kinds of people in the house. Nobody knew the number. What to do? I suspected and knew. I can't face Maharishi with a failure report. There was no 'can't', no 'impossible'. We had to achieve everything he had set out to do.' So, what to do? I didn't even have authorization to make outside calls.

Then I remembered I had the key to Mr. Ritterstaedt's office, where there was an outside line. So, I hurried over to the Kulm and called the national headquarters of the United States. That was a good idea. Luckily, there was already someone there; and I even knew this man from some courses, that was important, because telephone numbers were always a well-guarded thing in our Movement and were generally not allowed to be given out. I convinced the man that Maharishi needed the number and he gave it to me. I rushed back to the Sonnenberg. The WYMS believed me that I needed a line for Maharishi and I called Venezuela. Fortunately, Villanueva was actually there. I told him, 'Maharishi wants to talk to you, hold the line', and so, after half an hour of work, as if nothing had happened, I went with a cool face into the Gold Room and said to

Maharishi, 'Villanueva is on the line'. Maharishi also took this for granted and pressed the button to the hands-free speakerphone. I was in an emotional high. I felt that this was a decisive test and I had passed it. I had come up with something and had not given up.

Maharishi's personal secretary

One day, not too much later, Wolfgang Esch, who was the only active secretary at the time, came into my room and said, 'Maharishi asks if you want to help me in my job.' I thought, 'Not bad; that brings me closer to Maharishi,' and said, 'Yes.' In the evening, I was allowed to go to the suite. Maharishi asked me if I wanted to help Wolfgang: I said, 'Beautiful.'

It was only days later that I realized what this proposal meant. Wolfgang told me how it had come to this development. He had been introduced to the job a few months ago by the secretary Peter S., as his assistant. However, Peter became a Sidhi administrator soon after. He now had a different job, so that Wolfgang was alone.

The work could not be done by one person alone. From nine o' clock in the morning you had to be at the phone. If nobody called, you could meditate, but mostly you were disturbed. Later in the morning, the real work began and went on almost without interruption until late into the night: one o' clock, two o' clock were not uncommon.

Maharishi noticed of course that Wolfgang was completely overtired and exhausted. He said to him, 'Think about who could help you.' Wolfgang did not really feel like sharing his job with anyone, no matter how strenuous the work was. The constant contact with Maharishi was simply too rewarding, as was the privilege of the 'power' position, the recognition and admiration he enjoyed throughout Capital. Late in the evening, Maharishi asked again, 'Did you think of anyone who could help you?' Wolfgang told me that at that moment only the name 'Hans' came into his mind. Maharishi said, 'Hans will be very good.'

So, this is how I became Wolfgang's assistant. At least, it seemed that way. In fact, I was almost immediately the second secretary next to Wolfgang. Maharishi had meant it that way, but it was typical for him that he avoided any acknowledgement towards me, and thus also played down this promotion completely and quasi covered it up. Therefore, I only noticed it the next day or the day after next, when Wolfgang suddenly explained to me how to fold and unfold the antelope skin, which is spread out on Maharishi's seat. You have to know that the privilege of carrying the deer skin was the status symbol that showed that you were now one of Maharishi's two or three personal 'secretaries' and was thus, apparently, at the top of the Movement. In the Vedic-Indian tradition, Masters always sit on an antelope skin. Why that is, is not exactly known. A sensitive friend once explained to me that such a skin kept out negative earth rays and other vibrations. In our Movement, and so it was probably tradition, only the most trusted people, practically only the secretaries, were allowed to touch the deer skin.

So, when Wolfgang explained to me how to fold it, carry it behind the Master and spread it out on his seat, it suddenly became clear to me that I had now reached the top position.

Of course, in the beginning Wolfgang carried the deerskin, since he was senior to me. However, a few days later the time had come. I was on duty in the secretary's office, which was still inside the suite and Maharishi passed its door, which would open to the inside, when he went out. Wolfgang was not there. So, I took the deerskin and went behind Maharishi. The deerskin-bearer, as far as I remember, was generally allowed to join Maharishi into the narrow elevator cabin, where he tried to keep a maximum distance in order not to bother Maharishi with his less-developed vibes. Often, however, the secretary would rush down the two staircases by foot as the elevator glided down, receiving him at the bottom, and then walking down the long corridor diagonally behind Maharishi. In those days, there were usually still some staff members standing there who wanted to ask Maharishi something. When we walked down the gangway of the bridge to the Sonnenberg, at the side there stood Karl-Eberhard, called K.-E., an old friend of mine, and was one of the first to admire and envy my new status. In the evening, he jokingly told me, 'It is good that Maharishi finally has a secretary with a doctorate.'

From the bridge, we went through the gold room. Its back door was an entrance to the large and beautiful assembly hall, where the one to two hundred or so occupants of the 'Capital' were already waiting for Maharishi. In my excitement at the door, I did a stupid thing. The rule was that the deerskin-bearing secretary had to be the first to enter the hall to be able to lay out the skin in time. This way the people knew that Maharishi was right in front of the door and that they had to get up now. In this case, I somehow could not get past Maharishi in time because a relatively narrow alley of waiting people had formed outside. So, I asked him to let me pass. To disturb him in this way was of course not appropriate; but Maharishi smiled at me with understanding and walked aside knowing what a great moment this was for me.

I hurried to the stage and spread the fur on his seat. In the audience, I heard a surprised and admiring female voice shouting softly, 'Hans!' Until then, no one had known of my new status. I then went to the side in the background and waited until Maharishi had greeted those present by folding his hands, he sat down and folded in his legs to sit cross-legged. The ritual that followed then demanded that I go and push the little table in front of him. It was covered with golden brocade and had beautifully curved gilded legs. On top of it lay, always arranged by us beforehand, a stack of paper with gold edge and different colored felt-tip pens. Maharishi liked to scribble something on the paper as he spoke or listened, and sometimes took notes. There was also the gold-plated alarm clock that I had brought and set up together with the deerskin.

Maharishi almost never noticed the clock. Only when he felt that it was enough after very long sessions, usually during meditation, or bedtime, did he look at the clock and ended the session. When he pushed the table a little bit away from himself, the secretary, who had already discreetly moved on the stage from behind at the first sign of departure, went forward and pulled the table away completely, kneeling or crouching down so as not to obstruct Maharishi's view. Maharishi then got up, put his hands together in greeting, looking at everyone, and then walked to the steps that led sideways down to the back of the stage. At that moment, the secretary had to quickly fold the deerskin, clamp it under his arm, grab the written on papers and the alarm clock and hurry in behind Maharishi. He had to be careful not to be pushed away by the devotees. It would always be that Maharishi went to the next room for another meeting. There again the skin had to be spread out in time. This was the normal ritual of the meetings in the big hall, which I had often observed and in which I had always admired and envied the secretaries. I had the great good fortune to be able to take part in this ritual many more times, each time inwardly glowing and swelling with pride, but outwardly making myself as inconspicuous as possible. The secretary himself was not allowed to draw attention to himself!

Everything did not always go smoothly. Once, at a time when I was mentally miserable because I had the feeling that Maharishi was not satisfied with me, which was true, I actually let the skin drop on the floor in front of the sofa in the Gold Room when Maharishi was already standing directly behind me. Maharishi said, 'Oh'. That was terrible, because the deerskin was something like a holy object and was not allowed to touch the floor.

Another time, in the big hall, I had retreated as far as possible into the background as usual, being hidden by a ficus plant. When Maharishi stepped in front of the sofa, he looked to the side for a moment and noticed a figure behind the tree. He flinched, but then quickly caught himself after he recognized me. Of course, I was terribly embarrassed to have frightened Maharishi. That was the last thing I wanted and unconsciously the old worry came up in me that Maharishi might not quite trust me. In this situation, however, I also noticed that Maharishi was prone to have normal human reactions, which most of us at the time hardly thought possible, as we believed he was a divine being free from fear and virtually omniscient.

At my introductory meeting, Maharishi had given Wolfgang and me instructions on how to divide our work. He knew that none of us alone could endure a working day as long as his was. Therefore, we were to work in shifts so that everyone would get enough sleep and be able to do some 'program'. Maharishi said to us, 'Always do proper hopping (always do the flying program properly).' Obviously, it seemed that he reckoned that we would not be able to go through the other components, meditation and the other Sidhi Sutras, regularly.

Naturally, I left the better shift to Wolfgang. That was the late evening shift. In the evening and at night, Maharishi generally met special guests in the meeting room of his suite, and the secretaries were usually allowed to sit in, in case he needed anything or wanted to have someone call. The secretary could thus bathe in Maharishi's powerful yet loving charisma, and also be able to penetrate deeper into the Master's mind by listening. It was always very interesting what Maharishi thought about the different situations and areas of life.

I also tried to sit in at these meetings as long as I could. Only rarely did Maharishi admonish me to go to bed. He never said, 'Go to bed.' He only said, 'Go and rest.' Most of the time it was after midnight when I finally retired.

From nine in the morning I had to sit in the office, on a mat on the floor, the phones and intercoms set up around me. I then tried to meditate, because only rarely had I been able to do so earlier. This was a time when Maharishi did not like to be disturbed, for he too was meditating in his private room or at least he was in silence. This silence was felt to be very thick and full all the way to my office; it was a particularly blissful hour.

There were always disturbances, sometimes someone from the house wanted to know something, or someone called from outside, or perhaps an important person was leaving and Maharishi wanted to speak with the person before the departure. Every call tore me out of meditation, but I always hoped that it was something absolutely urgent, something about Maharishi wanted to be informed. So, I first had to find out what it was about and then decide if it could wait until later.

I had to be up to date; I had to know who was very important, who was reasonably important and who was less interesting. However, even someone in the third category could also have a significant and urgent thing running. I then tried to get a comprehensive picture of the project or issue in question, and to sense whether Maharishi would like to be disturbed for that matter or person.

When I felt that the matter could not be postponed, fortunately I was usually right. I was happy to call Maharishi and entered the secret number into the Intercom. At the other end, there was usually a very deep silence. I would whisper softly, 'Jai Guru Dev.' Most of the time Maharishi, who apparently had the intercom in front of him, answered in a very soft, almost frail voice: 'Jai Guru Dev'. Now I very gently and calmly presented the essence of what the caller wanted.

Then there were two possibilities. If Maharishi wanted to speak to the caller personally, then I put the call through to him. Immediately I would turn off the intercom so that I could not listen in, because I knew: Maharishi didn't like curiosity at all; any curious person was suspicious to him. I was allowed to know only as much as was necessary for my work. Any curious person was quickly suspected of being CIA.

Although in all my time in the Movement I never met anyone who was clearly a CIA member, Maharishi often talked about the 'CIA' – that was a synonym for 'the opposition.' I still do not know to this day whether he just wanted to train us or whether the CIA was actually already represented in our ranks. The fact was that the CIA, or related organizations, were monitoring our movement.

All groups that promote freedom of thought are a thorn in their eyes. And certainly, they have disrupted or even thwarted many of our projects. Later, when Maharishi enthusiastically spoke of some promising plan to even a slightly larger group such as: 'A government wants to introduce TM in the schools', or something like that, I already knew. It won't work anyway; it is just a diversion for the 'CIA.' And indeed, all these projects were somehow disrupted or thwarted at the last minute. The really important projects, on the other hand, were always announced only after they had already been carried out.

If, on the other hand, Maharishi didn't want to talk to the caller privately, he would give me instructions over the intercom what to say to the person, either while he was still connected or later. I had to be careful that the caller was muted first, so they could not listen in. Once I made the mistake of just covering the receiver with my hand while Maharishi made a remark. Then Maharishi suddenly asked, 'Did he hear that? Ask him.' In fact, through my hand the caller had understood what Maharishi had said. This, in turn, he had obviously felt and noticed. Of course, he was angry and rebuked me.

Another very interesting situation arose whenever Maharishi wanted to talk directly to the other person via the intercom, for which purpose I switched his phone to hands-free mode. Then I could hear both sides and sometimes I could intervene clarifying if one or the other side did not understand correctly. However, it could become nerve-racking if a third person called on another phone at the same time, whom I had to question and 'handle' very quietly.

I had a slight suspicion that one of the reasons Maharishi was conducting these conversations over the intercom in this way was so that I could learn something. These were not the most confidential things that were discussed, but they were sometimes extremely revealing. Let me tell you about two such conversations: Once two 'Governors', i. e. TM teachers, travelled around Africa on Maharishi's behalf and established contacts. These two had been invited to lunch by the President of a country the following day. After they had received instructions from Maharishi on how to conduct the conversation, they asked, 'Surely there will be meat at the lunch. What should we do? Eat out of courtesy?' Maharishi just said, 'It's too late.' They repeated their question. He said again, 'It's too late.' Neither they nor I knew what to do with that answer. I intervened and tried to make the situation clear to Maharishi. But, he had understood very well. He explained, 'It is too late to ask such questions. We do not eat poison just to please a friend.'

Another very funny situation was the following: The caller was Bruno Romano, the Italian National Leader of our movement. Toward the end of the conversation, which had been about national activities, Maharishi suddenly touched upon the Colosseum in Rome. He said that Bruno should go to the mayor of Rome and tell him to tear down that horrible building where people had been thrown to the lions in those days.

Bruno was struck dumb. Finally, he was able to argue that millions, or even billions, of dollars had been spent to run the subway under the Coliseum without damaging it. Maharishi was not impressed. He said, 'Go to the mayor and tell him that you had a friend from abroad visiting. He found Rome wonderful. Only when he came to the Coliseum he had exclaimed: 'What a terribly gloomy building! You can still feel the terrible cruelty that took place there! The building should definitely be torn down!'

Such challenges by Maharishi to his students were typical. He wanted to make us strong through things like this. Imagine how poor Bruno must have felt during his audience with the mayor! If he only had the courage to comply with Maharishi's wish! As mentioned earlier, Maharishi always made a point of speaking at the last minute to important guests who were leaving, as well as to close associates who were going on a special mission. On the one hand, the departing guests were happy to speak to Maharishi in person, but on the other hand, it put their nerves to the test. Especially since Maharishi had the habit of always appearing at the very last minute or being connected at the very last minute.

Usually it went like this: I knew when the person had to leave at the latest and arranged drivers, cars, luggage transport, etc. The person would then wait for at an internal phone or in the meeting room. In time, I cautiously reminded Maharishi that so-and-so had to leave immediately and was waiting for him. Maharishi then said something like, 'Yes, I am coming.' But then it usually took quite some time until he actually appeared. He did not want people to waste their time and energy waiting at the airport.

So, he usually only came out of his room when the person, according to our calculations, should have left. Then he spoke to them calmly. Those who had experienced this a few times before, could relax knowing that if they left it to Maharishi, they would reach their flight. Maharishi would close the conversation at just the right moment, so the traveler would arrive at the airport at the last minute. If someone arrived at the terminal well after the departure time, it almost always turned out that the plane was also delayed. If someone was participating in this ritual for the first time, one could assume that he or she was going through quite a lot during that hour, in his or her favour, of course, because the excitement released a lot of stress.

Regarding Maharishi's conversations with the departing guests, I would like to tell a nice story that happened only after I was no longer secretary. I heard it from Deepak Chopra, and that only on a video tape. Deepak is now known worldwide as a spiritual author, speaker and seminar leader. What perhaps not everyone knows is that Maharishi built him up.

Deepak had learned TM and was a devotee of Maharishi. After some time of training, Maharishi sent him on frequent tours to give lectures on TM and Maharishi's approach to world peace. Once Deepak wanted to visit his family in India. As usual, Maharishi wanted to see him again just before his departure. As usual, the meeting took place at the last minute, actually already too late. Nevertheless, Maharishi was calm and talked to Deepak at length. He instructed him to contact a number of top politicians in India and present the new Ayurvedic health approach of TM to them. Deepak was a doctor by training. So that fitted very well.

Deepak was used to Maharishi's habits, but nevertheless he thought in silence, 'How am I supposed to get to all these top politicians in the short time of my stay in India, which is already so crowded anyway?' The conversation dragged on endlessly, until the flight was definitely departed. Deepak thought, 'Should I even go to the airport now?' But he went anyway in order to catch at least the next flight. When he arrived at the airport, it turned out that the plane had been delayed for several hours and that Deepak's seat had already been given to someone else. They apologized to him many times and offered him a seat in business class. Of course, Deepak did not object.

Only one more passenger flew in this class, an Indian. The two got into conversation and Deepak told him in detail about the Vedic approach to health of the Master. After some time, the fellow traveler said, 'The fact that I met you here is a gift from heaven. After all, I am on a mission for the Indian government and was supposed to be researching new promising health care systems in the West. And I must say: I had not found anything worth reporting so far. In the next few days, I have meetings with the President, the Minister of Health and some other politicians and representatives of the health authorities. Would you be ready to come along and present your approach? It seems to me to be the only really new and promising one, and that it comes originally from India!'

So now, Deepak had his presentations, with exactly the people Maharishi had told him to contact, without any trouble! This was one of those miracles that one experienced again and again when working with Maharishi.

The situations in which Maharishi came out of his room early in the morning and where I could walk along the still silent corridor behind him, with the deerskin under my arm, were among the most joyful moments for me. Maharishi was then still so fresh and in the silence; it was pure bliss.

Of course, it was even better when I could sit with him at the meeting that followed. I had to develop a fine feeling for whether this was appropriate. Often the meetings were too confidential or too personal. Then I waited outside the room to see whether Maharishi would call me.

In the beginning, I misjudged the situation once and did not realize that Maharishi did not want me in the room. I must have missed a respective gesture and he accosted me sternly: 'Get out!' That was a real stab in the heart; although I was sure it was for my own good. But Maharishi never held a grudge against anyone; after the session he was as friendly as ever.

After I had sat in the office for a few hours in the morning, and especially when something was on, I realized that I was missing meditation and especially 'hopping'. I then waited anxiously for Wolfgang to take over the job. But he usually took his time, because he almost always stayed with Maharishi until late into the night. When he finally came, I went into the basement to meditate a little bit and to do my 'Sidhi' program. Afterwards Wolfgang and I were mostly active at the same time. During the day there was always something going on. We had to arrange meetings for Maharishi, wait outside the door of the meeting room in case something was needed or someone was called in. Telephone calls came in as well as inquiries from the house itself. Everyone came to us with the request to 'check' something.

Maharishi always managed to keep many, many staff members or project groups in suspense at the same time. Very often, projects came to a point where Maharishi had to give a new instruction or where a new direction was needed. Often people were sitting on 'pins and needles' because external negotiators were waiting for a response. But Maharishi, as always, had the peace of mind. You should not think that we could always ask Maharishi any question we wanted. Not at all. He was constantly busy with the conversations and meetings that he wanted to have. There was seldom an opportunity to bring up other things.

So, Wolfgang and I wrote down all questions to be asked of Maharishi with all details in a booklet. Maharishi had advised us to do this. We both hoped to receive as many serious and important questions as possible. Which of us got which project was apparently subject to chance, depending on which of us was on the phone or was approached by a questioner on his way through the house. However, if a project group had already checked something through one of us, they usually went back to the person who already knew the background.

With small things, we could give instructions if we thought we knew Maharishi's opinion about it or felt it clearly. Nevertheless, we had to be very careful, because Maharishi wanted to know about everything and keep everything under control. It was not so much about the projects themselves, but about the fact that the people through their project were inwardly aligned with him.

Both of us had an interest in handling as many projects as possible, because it gave us the chance to talk to Maharishi more often. The 'disadvantage' was that each time we 'checked' something, Maharishi gave us new work, instructions on what to do and how to handle the project. That was fine with us. The more jobs each of us had, the more chances we had to report about the progress and success of our work.

Every conversation with Maharishi, no matter how small, was simply bliss. When the rare opportunity came to present questions, sometimes it took days or, on rare occasions, more than a week to get a decision, the complexity of the project had already reduced enormously by itself. What had been a huge story at the beginning could be summed up in two sentences. And, in a few minutes Maharishi gave a direction that the questioners could then follow up for weeks.

In this way, Maharishi kept countless people on their toes at the same time. During the waiting time, they had also released a lot of 'stress' and lost their nervousness and worry. I don't remember any case where a serious project was really damaged because people didn't get the answer in time, even if it seemed to them that the world was about to collapse at any moment. We were always able to ask at the last second, and they got their directive.

And what kind of projects were involved? One of the wildest was that we wanted to build a chip factory. We even bought some really expensive machinery. Money didn't matter to Maharishi in such things, while on the other hand he almost pedantically trained us to save in all corners and get the very best prices everywhere. He was able to invest a hundred thousand dollars in a project that ultimately served only to train one person, and at the same time demand that we collect at least three price quotes for pencils!

To build the chip factory we had to find meditating engineers from all over the world and inspire them to come to Seelisberg. And indeed, quite a few did come. It seems to me that in the end the real purpose was to get new people in Maharishi's vicinity who wanted to work for him. Because when the project was put on the 'back burner' at some point, as had long been foreseen, most of them stayed on and did other jobs.

Similar to the chip factory, a production of quartz wristwatches, a new technology at that time, was to be started. However, this project did not get beyond the planning stage. But it was different with the Tape Factory, a factory in which the video tapes that were constantly being sent to all centers were to be produced. At that time, our organization was the second largest purchaser of video master tapes and U-matic cassettes in Europe (or even worldwide). Maharishi saw a huge potential for savings. In fact, a gigantic factory was purchased second-hand and installed in a building in the neighboring village of Emmetten. We also bought the technology for $100,000.

The leaders of our project were Peter P. and Jost H. When the factory had been set up and started after a lot of work, it turned out that it did not produce usable tapes. The purchased technology was obviously inadequate. Magnetic tape is a medium for magnetic recording, and is made of a thin, magnetizable coating of iron oxide on a long, narrow strip of plastic film. The main problem was that the thin layer containing the magnetic coating quickly wore off the film base when it passed over a video recorder's playback head many times. Peter and Jost now had to do their own experiments to prolong the so-called still-frame time, the time the tape in the still-frame withstood the constant wearing of the head over the same spot. However, the two did not make any progress; the tapes produced remained useless.

Finally, Maharishi intervened more intensively, and I could observe the pragmatism he displayed here as well. He met Peter and Jost every day in his suite, in the small meeting room where I had worked with Heiner R. before. There Maharishi asked them to hang diagrams, charts, with all aspects and parameters they were experimenting with on the wall. Maharishi instructed them to change only one parameter per run (for example, the time it took to wear off the iron oxide coating) and to leave everything else the same. Every day he listened to the results, had them written on the charts (e.g., 'still-frame 5 minutes') and gave instructions on which parameter to change next.

Day after day, they reported on the respective results, some of which naturally included a deterioration in quality, until after about three weeks a usable tape with good image quality and a still-frame of many hours was produced. This achievement was only due to Maharishi's wisdom.

But now comes the doozy. The tapes have never been used! As soon as the factory was up and running, Maharishi said that it should be transported as a whole to another country, probably India. So, the machines and conveyor belts were dismantled, carefully packed in plastic film and then taken to a duty-free warehouse. And there they remained until after about 10 years. In order to save storage fees, they were then shipped to our new 'Capital' in Vlodrop in Holland, where they were put in a special room and sealed by customs. Perhaps they are still lying there today. Did Maharishi have this in mind from the beginning? I do not think that this is impossible. Maybe he had started the whole project just for the 'development' of those involved.

One of the standard and favorite projects that Maharishi engaged his followers in was to find real estate. All over the world, he inspired Governors to look for either large buildings that could be used as TM academies, or a site on which to build an academy. Again and again,

Wolfgang and I received calls from someone who had found a very suitable and cheap old hotel. We knew that Maharishi was very interested in such a thing. Then we had to ask for all the details, and if we thought we had a complete picture of the land or building, we were happy to have a serious reason to call Maharishi via intercom.

We didn't realize at the time that these projects were in large part just an excuse to keep people busy and put them in difficult negotiation situations, for example, where they could become stronger. This was very simple, especially with the question of the purchase price. In most cases, our people had already held preliminary negotiations and received a good offer. But no matter how low it was, the standard was that Maharishi said we should offer half; sometimes it was even less.

This often put our negotiators in embarrassing situations, because our offer seemed really ridiculous. Also, Maharishi always asked for details that no one had thought to inquire about. So, in this way he also trained us, Wolfgang and me. Over the time, we had each worked out checklists for ourselves, according to which we asked the callers about: size, location, construction, environment… But no matter how much detailed information we had prepared, Maharishi practically always asked about something we hadn't considered, e.g., 'Is it carpeted?' 'Oh, I'm sorry, I don't know.' 'Then find out.'

And so, we had something to do again, had to make calls and so on. It was always the same game. The hotels, I think, were very rarely actually bought.

Through these projects, the master was also fooling the public. Apparently, he made a point of making the world think that his organization was infinitely rich, which it definitely was not. We devotees always believed we had to defend Maharishi when others thought he was greedy for money. But he didn't care about such things, on the contrary, he promoted the image of the infinitely rich guru who was only after money.

I remember a very crazy meeting one evening in the gold room. An Indian journalist had arrived and wanted to write a report about us. Because he was Indian, we all thought that he would report favourably about us.

Maharishi granted him access to all departments (certainly in generous doses), and in the evening he was allowed to attend a supposedly highly confidential meeting in the closest circle. I, who was not yet secretary at that time, and other staff members were present as extras. But of course, I did not know what was about to happen, I was only surprised about the completely wild course of events. Every few minutes a 'very important' call came in from somewhere in the world, and someone reported about a hotel he had found. Maharishi asked about the purchase price without delay and then suggested an offer that we should make. The amount was just being tossed back and forth in the millions.

The journalist took a lot of photos and wrote everything down. He did not work for the Indian press as we had thought. Later a big, very critical article written by him appeared in the Stern, in which he reported attending a very secret meeting. He would have noticed that Maharishi was only interested in real estate and money. So that is what the show was for!

All in all, Wolfgang's and my days were a string of pearls of pure moments of happiness. All our thinking revolved around Maharishi. When is there a good reason to call him? Does he give us special orders, about the success of which we could then report again? When does he come out of his suite, so that we could walk behind him with the deerskin (and then be admired as great secretaries)? When does he call us to get some people to come to meetings? When are there big meetings or 'boat rides' that we have to organize?

We worked until we were exhausted, but we were in constant bliss for that very reason. Only rarely was there an opportunity to recover through a little meditation. I remember that once I could retreat to the secretaries' room because I knew that Wolfgang was taking care of Maharishi who was holding some kind of meeting in one of the meeting rooms. I sat down on my mattress, around me, as usual several telephones, and started to meditate. I immediately fell into an almost comatose state of exhaustion. Suddenly one of the telephones started ringing. I somehow sensed that it was Wolfgang who needed support. I heard the phone, and then the other one too, ringing right next to me, and they rang and rang, but I was so completely exhausted that I could practically not move. I just had to let them ring and continued, half awake, half asleep, to think the mantra. This working to the point of collapse was obviously a training program of Maharishi, through which our blockages and resistance were loosened. I had already had such extreme training in the video department.

The Battle of 'Weissenhauser Beach'

One or two months after I started working as a secretary, it was between Christmas 1978 and New Year 1979, one early morning I was assigned a special mission, which should prove to be quite an adventure. I later called it by myself 'the Battle of Weissenhauser Beach.' Maharishi called me on the intercom. I was to fly to Weissenhauser Beach Resort in Northern Germany with top lady, N. There, the last part of the first Sidhi Center course was just beginning, which Heiner R. and I had been working on preparing until recently.

In Schleswig-Holstein, more than 1,500 participants were to come together to learn the final technique, Yogic Flying. I quickly packed my suitcase. That day it was incredibly warm, hairdryer weather, certainly above plus 15° Celsius. I seriously considered whether I should take my winter coat with me, and did so despite the warmth, you never know. But I did not take a cap. I was driven to the airport, where our Centurion, a single-engine propeller plane with four seats, was already waiting for me. N. had not made it in time and was to follow by train with several helpers.

So I flew with two pilots over the sunny German countryside to Kiel and was picked up there by car and taken to my hotel. Until then I did not really know, what my task would be. From the hotel, I talked to Maharishi, who explained to me what it was all about, checking the finances of the course participants. For many of them 'International' had not yet received the course fees, even though they had all supposedly already paid. The instructions were not to take place until all finances were cleared. My task was to work with all of them, talk to participants whose tuition fees had not yet shown up and find out where the money might have gone. N. and her 'finance-ladies' were then to go through the bank statements again. I got a TM teacher to help me, Bernd Nothelle. That whole day we both sat together with the different problem candidates and then gave N. our information, so that practically all missing amounts could be found.

After one or two days, Bernd and I travelled to the nearby island of Fehmarn, where a second part of the course were staying. N. and her ladies remained at the Weißenhauser Beach resort, on the mainland. In the evening, we were to bring her our results. Bernd and I had worked the whole day. In the course of the day, the weather worsened seriously. It began to storm. Finally, the weather was so strong that we had trouble getting from one house to another. The houses, in which our people lived, formed a row and were separated by gaps. When we stepped out of the door of one of these houses, the wind that whistled through the gap simply blew us away and we had to crawl up to the next house.

It then became freezing cold and started snowing heavily. When we finished our work at midnight and wanted to return to our headquarters, Bernd said, 'Shouldn't we wait until tomorrow morning? Driving through the night in this storm is dangerous. Tomorrow might be better weather.' I said, 'No, we have to get the results to N. immediately so she can have everything checked that very night.'

The journey was indeed adventurous. When we drove over the bridge to the mainland, snowdrifts were already building across the road every few meters, luckily from the left, so that our roadway was still passable. At Weissenhauser Beach the snow was already so deep that we could only get to our hotel up to about 50 meters distance, then we were stuck and had to walk. It became clear. If we had left even only half an hour later, we would not have come back and would have been stuck on Fehmarn for many days.

I immediately went to N. It was about one or two o' clock in the morning, and knocked to get her out of bed. Her helpers had to process our results immediately. But N. convinced me to let her girls sleep. They had worked through several nights and could not do any more. I felt myself soften. However, that was a mistake, as it turned out the next morning. When I spoke to Maharishi on the phone, he was very angry. The bank statements should have been checked immediately, because today was Friday, the last day before the weekend, when the students could have called their banks for remaining uncertainties.

It may seem here as if Maharishi was only after the money. But that was certainly not the point. In fact, he had the teachings given the next day, although not everything had been clarified yet. Rather, I suspect it was cosmically important that before such an important initiation and strategic action, as I will explain in a moment, all material matters were in order. It was also about my training. I should have remained clear and strong in my decision and put his concern first, despite all other considerations.

The next day the extreme weather continued: a hurricane-like storm, icy cold around −16° Celsius and snow, snow, snow. After a short time, we were cut off from the outside world. The snowdrifts accumulated up to the roof of the houses, sometimes even higher. We did not have to starve, because the organizers had apparently bought enough food for the whole course. But we had great difficulty getting from one house to the other. It was lucky that I had my winter coat with me. For a hat, I wrapped a towel around my head. I had never experienced such bad weather, and probably the others hadn't either.

Many villages in the surrounding area were completely snowed in. The train had not been able to run for a long time. Later I saw pictures of how the tracks were cleared after the storm, buried several meters deep under the snow in some places. Only helicopters were able to bring food to the villages and transport sick people when the worst of the storm was over.

In fact, it was already well known within our Movement, and it became apparent several times later, that outside temperatures often dropped significantly, where we held our Courses. Maharishi, supported by his physicists, explained that orderliness was associated with low temperatures. Low temperatures meant less disordered movement of molecules and atoms. Extremely low temperatures, close to absolute zero, would result in the superconductivity of metals and the superfluidity of helium, which in physics was interpreted as perfect order and coherence of all particles involved. Maharishi explained that during meditation, and especially through the practice of Sidhis and Yogic Flying, the coherence,

i. e., the orderliness of consciousness increases, which has actually been shown by the greater order of the brain waves. Inner silence reduces the 'mental temperature', so to speak. Since consciousness and matter are closely related, indeed, in modern physics they are understood as identical in a certain manner, the mental coherence of larger meditation groups increases the coherence in the environment, and that simply means increasing coldness.

Many years later I heard from a German career officer[*17] that in September 1978 the biggest military maneuvers on both sides of the German border took place in that area, indicating an imminent conflict between NATO and the Warsaw Pact. The officer himself had taken part in NATO maneuvers in Schleswig-Holstein, the Northern district at the Baltic Sea. Maharishi had visited inside the German border and had travelled as far as Fehmarn. For an invasion of Germany, the USSR fleet lying in the Baltic Sea would have had to pass through the narrow shipping passage between Germany and Denmark near Fehmarn, which was frozen during the TM course. In addition, air, rail and road traffic was completely paralyzed for several days.

In December, Maharishi said: 'There is an iron sword hanging on a silken thread over Germany. Every meditator in Germany should go to the course in Fehmarn and learn the Sidhis and yogic flying.'

When the students told him about the extreme cold wave at the end of the course, he said, 'We changed a world catastrophe into a natural catastrophe.' When the military archives of the Warsaw Pact became accessible to the public in the 1990s, experts actually found Warsaw Pact plans for nuclear attacks on Munich, Stuttgart, Frankfurt, Bonn, Cologne, Brussels, Amsterdam and two sites in Denmark. On August 13, 2008, the 'Frankfurter Allgemeine Zeitung' reported in detail about the planned nuclear war in Europe.

My theory is: Maharishi had the Course set near the inhospitable Baltic Sea to prevent an invasion. During the natural disaster, an invasion was of course, out of the question. No tank would have gotten very far now. Otherwise, he did not like the Baltic Sea at all when it came to Courses. When the year after, the national director, Mrs. Eickhoff, wanted to organize a big Course at the same place again, he was absolutely against it, in spite of intensive pressure from Mrs. Eickhoff.

At some point, even before the Course was over, the weather calmed down and the two pilots were able to go with me to Kiel airport. During the flight, I experienced something that was not right. For some reason the left door of our Centurion could not shut properly. After we took off, we could only circle one lap and then had to land again. The pilots tied the door to the opposite pilot's seat with a rope, and then we took off again. But due to the strong suction during the flight, the door opened again by a gap of about 5 cm, right next to me. I gradually became cold, so I stuffed my grey winter coat into this slit to keep the cold air out. This went well for a while, but as we rose in altitude, suddenly my coat was pulled completely out of the plane by the suction. At the last second, I was able to grab a corner and pull the coat back in with all my effort. Imagine if anyone on the ground had suddenly seen a grey winter coat floating from the sky that winter evening! Perhaps a freezing homeless person who could have accepted this as a sign from heaven. Maybe it would have converted him to the faith!

When I arrived in Seelisberg, another, not so pleasant surprise was waiting for me. My room was under water, or better, had been under water. After my departure, the weather had changed here as well. The storm had opened my window. When it froze afterwards, the water pipe in my room burst. The flooding that followed was particularly catastrophic inasmuch as I, ascetic as I was, slept only on a foam rubber mattress a few centimeters thick and a support board like one that sometimes provides the backing for wardrobes. Also, all my things were stored on the floor, including my sacred books. So, of course, everything was completely drenched and ruined.

That was my 'Battle of the Weissenhauser Beach', with many days of very little sleep, always cheering up and encouraging the 'men', and further privations, as they were normal ingredients of a 'war'.

Maharishi sent me a few more times on 'special missions', for example, once to Kühtai in the Tyrolean Alps and twice to Vienna. On the flight to Tyrol, I had the fantastic pleasure of sitting in the cockpit of the

Citation and enjoying the view of the mountain valleys below me. These assignments, like all projects, were not only practical necessities for me, but, perhaps even more importantly, for my 'training'.

In Kühtai, for example, I came across an old pattern of mine. As soon as the job was reasonably complete, it pulled me back 'home' as quickly as possible. That was the same here. When I thought my work was finished, I called Maharishi. However, by asking some questions, he quickly found out that not everything was completed yet. This was quite embarrassing for me, because I had already had the respective feeling of completion. So, I had to stay another day or two. Everybody else would have been glad to have a holiday in this beautiful mountain world, but I was fixated on the fastest possible return. On a trip a few weeks later, another test was waiting for me in Vienna that I unfortunately did not quite pass; and this is still bothering me today.

In Kühtai, there was an Austrian TM-teacher in the core group about whom I got the impression that he was undermining and sabotaging the Movement. Back in Seelisberg, I told Maharishi that I suspected this teacher was a Communist. Maharishi instructed me to tell this man that he was a Communist, which at the time meant he was from the 'other' side.

Now you must know that I was quite afraid of being rejected, especially by a larger group, and Maharishi certainly felt that. It was likely that I would not make myself popular. And so, during my next visit I falsified the task by saying that Maharishi had said that he was a Communist. That was not good at all because it was clear to us secretaries that we should not bring Maharishi into any negative context and associations. By the way, even with this accusation, everyone was totally against me; they defended the 'good and reliable co-worker' and were now not only against me but also against Maharishi. This situation was very difficult for me, and I felt that Maharishi had certainly intended this.

By the way, I was surprised that he sent me, as a German, to Austria several times to get things going or to put things in order there. I took this as an indication that he regarded the Germans and the Austrians as one people.

On the whole, I seemed to be doing my job quite well, and Maharishi seemed satisfied with me, although he never gave me the slightest credit. On the contrary, for example it was later in India, Mr. Goenka, the manager of the 'Indian Express' newspaper, mentioned in my presence how prudent and clever Hans regulated everything. Maharishi offhandedly made the pun: 'Lufthansa' (In India they wrote my name 'Hansa'). Apparently, he wanted to prevent me from becoming too vain. Some others, however, he praised to excess and blew up their egos like a balloon until it was about to burst. This was almost embarrassing for all outsiders, only the person concerned did not notice it in general. My pride, on the other hand, was nourished precisely by the fact that I obviously did not need such exaggerated acclamation.

On the other hand, I remember one time when he praised me indirectly, hidden in a heavy rebuke. The thing was that even as a secretary I was still in charge of the video department. One of my tasks was to make sure that the KSCI,[18] our own television station in the USA, would regularly receive a current video tape with a lecture by Maharishi every week. Once Maharishi was absent for a few weeks and, and had told the head of the video library, Alfred B., that he should not release any video tape from his library at all until further notice. When I asked Alfred to send a tape to the KSCI, as usual, he said, 'I'm not allowed to do that, direct order from Maharishi!' Arguing did not help. What could I do? I could not reach Maharishi. In this case, I felt that I really could not do anything. And even after he had returned, I never managed to talk to him about this matter. It seemed to me that I just had to relax. KSCI had to figure out how to fill that gap in their program.

Then, one day, at least two months had already passed, the head of KSCI, Walter Koch, came to Seelisberg to discuss the general situation of his station. One evening, very late in the night, a meeting took place in Maharishi's small meeting room. I was there, and at an appropriate moment, I mentioned that the station had not received its regular tape for weeks. When Maharishi heard this, he exploded and verbally beat me to a pulp. I tried to defend myself, by reminding him that he had instructed Alfred not to send tapes, but Maharishi did not accept anything. He just kept on ranting; it hit me like a surge of energy. Wolfgang, who was sitting next to me, noticed the power as well and became very small. Maharishi said something like, 'Such a foolishness! I have relied on you so much! You have such a good education! You are on top of the movement and now you are letting me down like that! If I am not here and can't be asked, you don't dare to make decisions…'

So basically, he praised me implicitly! But I was completely devastated and thought, 'Now he's sending me home.' Finally, he said, 'Now go and rest!' I went out, but I couldn't go to bed yet, because I was responsible for driving Walter to his hotel, as it was far after midnight and nobody was up.

When Walter finally came and we were sitting in the car together, I was still embarrassed. Walter tried to comfort me by telling me that he himself had said to Maharishi after I left, 'But he is very sincere.' Maharishi had said, 'Yes, I know.' The next day, I was still in shock. I had some things to organize in the big hall. I had obviously not been sent home yet, when Maharishi suddenly came along, apparently on his way to a meeting. I put my hands together in greeting. Against his habit, he stopped, greeted me as well, and said to me as if he wanted to keep me informed, which he usually never did, 'I go and meet these people.'

I had no idea whom he wanted to meet, but that was not the point. Maharishi just wanted to calm me down and take the depression off me that he obviously felt. He showed to me that he was not in the least bit resentful and had already left last night's affair completely behind him. But then why had he squeezed me so hard? He had put me in this hopeless situation himself, probably even consciously! I am quite sure that he wanted to do something good for me. Maybe he wanted to lure my old fear of recrimination to the surface. Or maybe he even wanted to take old karma from me, that is what the Masters do, as we all know. Anyway, after this event I was very relieved.

Crisis

Unfortunately, there was also a period when Maharishi was obviously not satisfied with me, and I didn't even know why. One day he had a meeting with Wolfgang, me, K.-E. and Uwe, the two who were responsible for the production of printed materials. The four of us were to form a new team to manage the entire communications of the 'Capital'. Wolfgang was to make telephone calls to all countries of the world, I was to read all incoming letters and give instructions on how they should be answered, by a team that I would be assigned to. My heart contracted, although the new job sounded very honorable. I thought, 'What a pity, it seems that my secretarial job is coming to an end. Now I'm just a floorwalker.'

But since one did everything the Master wanted without asking much, I threw myself into the new task during the days after. The job kept me on my toes from early morning to late afternoon. I was given the 'White Room' with my crew, where each of my people had their own table with a typewriter. I read all incoming official mail; the private mail I sorted into the appropriate mailboxes. I handed the mail addressed to individual departments to their representatives, who came to me once a day. I had to do everything myself and was not allowed to delegate anything. Then I gave instructions to all the country secretaries on how to answer the letters, read their letters, corrected them and, if necessary, had them rewritten.

It was a huge task. In the afternoon at 5 o' clock, when everyone went to do their 'program', I was pretty exhausted and also went to meditate. After all, I was obviously no longer Maharishi's personal secretary. Wolfgang understood his job differently. He continued to linger at Maharishi's door, wherever he was and used the phones that were at different places for his calls. When Maharishi went somewhere else, Wolfgang took the deerskin as usual and followed him. Wolfgang still saw himself as a secretary.

I did my new job with all my heart and soul and I certainly did it very well. But more and more I felt that Maharishi was not satisfied with me. He did not smile at me anymore, yes, he looked away or at the floor when he passed me. What was I doing wrong? I did exactly what he had told me!

This dragged on for a whole series of weeks. I became increasingly unhappy, even desperate. Surely, I could have asked Wolfgang for advice, but somehow, I did not think of it, especially since I was a bit angry that he took his new assignment so easily and only took it as a sideline to his secretary position.

One day I came out of the White Room again at 5 o' clock and happened to walk past the 'Pink Room' where Maharishi obviously had a meeting. Wolfgang stayed in front of the door. I stood around with him for a while. Then Wolfgang said, 'Hans, I am quite tired and would like to meditate a little. Could you possibly stay here, in case Maharishi wants something?'

'Okay,' I said, with some misgivings. Did Maharishi even want me to be his secretary anymore? Anyway, I stayed. At some point Maharishi rang the bell. I went in feeling a little uneasy. How would he react if I came in instead of Wolfgang? However, he acted very coolly and gave me a small order, to get some materials. After that, he rang for me several times and gave me orders for a meeting in the evening, to which I should invite various people.

When he rang again and I came in, I saw that he was getting up. Was I now allowed to take his deerskin as before? There was no one else there. So, I did and watched him as I was doing it. Apparently, he did not mind. I went over the bridge to the Kulm, with the deerskin, behind him. At that moment Wolfgang came back from his meditation; he stood at the side, greeted Maharishi, smiled at me afterwards and nodded in agreement. He was obviously really happy that I had taken up my position again, although he had been able to enjoy Maharishi's increased attention since I had held myself back. I have never forgotten his joy at my happiness, which showed his true friendship.

There was no more time for meditation for me now. I scurried around and organized everything for the evening meeting. Once I was about to leave the Gold Room, I saw Maharishi was already at the door. I held the door open for him. Then he beamed at me, and I suddenly and finally realized what had gone wrong all this time. It was not that I should have given up the secretarial position. No, I had just been given an additional task: the management of the White Room. I had not imagined this before, because the new job was more than a full-time job. But Maharishi thought differently than a normal boss. He knew how much he could get me to do without me breaking down completely. He wanted to push me to my limits and force me to become more effective, because now I had to find ways to double my productivity.

From that moment on, I no longer cared about my regular 'program', apart from the short 'hopping' sessions Maharishi had recommended. I was there only for him, which put me in constant high spirits even more than before. I also found ways to combine my two tasks, for example, by always carrying all the mail I had to read and process in a small suitcase. Whenever I had to wait in front of the room, where Maharishi was meeting people, I would open the suitcase and read the letters. This was not easy, because I had to distinguish between the different categories, such as unread or already edited documents in the suitcase.

It also became difficult when Maharishi called me, because then I had to quickly gather everything together, stuff it into the suitcase and rush in with it in my hand. But I got used to it. From then on, everything was fine again. Maharishi was obviously satisfied and gave me his full attention.

India – climax and crash

These two wonderful years faded away. Now and then Maharishi traveled; sometimes we knew where to go, sometimes not. After all, we were not the highest VIPs. There was the Indian secretary, Nandkishore, and there were the top ladies, some of whom were more 'in' than we were.

One day a bigger journey was ahead again, to India. As usual, we had only a faint idea of what it was all about. Anyway, it was our job to get the plane tickets. Apparently, the whole leadership elite was supposed to go on the flight. There was, as so often happens, a total back and forth about who was allowed to fly and who was not. This kept a lot of people in a state of excitement.

In several meetings, Maharishi went through the names with Wolfgang and me. We negotiated with different airlines and finally ordered the tickets, spread over different days and flights. The very highest elite group flew last, and also first class. Again, there were meetings where everything was thrown overboard. No, this one stays here, he flies later, but this one and this one goes with him.

Again, and again we had to call the airline and change the bookings, until they got completely out of hand and told us. If you change anything else, we are not going to do it again. Then we would have to fly with another airline. Wolfgang and I also waited with excitement until the last moment waiting for the decision whether we should come along or stay to maintain operations. Finally, Maharishi told us, 'Yes, you're going too.' Great joy! And we asked Maharishi, 'On what flight do you yourself fly?' 'I'm not flying, I'm staying here,' he said. Big disappointment! So, we should be hanging out in India without Maharishi? But, unfortunately I couldn't ask for the reason.

At the very last minute, with the approval of the airline, we had the final list ready. I sat next to our telex operator and dictated it to him. When the list was submitted, I threw myself flat on the floor in exhaustion and relief. Somehow, I was thrilled to be allowed to go to India, even though Maharishi might not come along. Wolfgang was not on the list and so he stayed back after all. I was supposed to be the tour guide of the main flight.

Like Wolfgang, I had just gotten a movement car, a big Pontiac, because we could get it cheaply from the USA. I was very proud. So far, I had only driven it once. The trip to the airport was my second and, as it turned out later, my last tour with it. I am sure Maharishi knew that. The car was simply used for the movement, and to feed my ego, he had assigned it to me. I had to stop by our contract gas station the morning of departure to refuel with our own 'currency', which was in reality something like gas coupons. But the gas station was only open for a certain time. Besides, the Pontiac was quite slow and cumbersome. I arrived very late at the airport with all the tickets. During the night, there had been several changes. The corresponding tickets had to be redone; even the local head of the airline took part in this, as the movement secretaries could not have done it on their own.

At this point, I suddenly had to make a decision. One of the top ladies who was to fly first class had been taken off the list. Who was to get her first-class seat now? My first reaction was, 'Then I, as secretary, group leader and therefore important person, could take this preferred seat.' But fortunately, following this impulse was a somewhat queasy feeling. I gave the seat to another top lady who would otherwise have flown economy class. What I did not know at that time was that our travel service agent, Willi Kempe, later had to tell the Master about my choice. He then said, as I heard it from Willi, 'That was a good decision.' Well, I was glad to have held myself back!

From Zurich, we were supposed to go to Paris, in order to change to the intercontinental flight there. I, as a tour guide and officially director of our travel, had no idea what was going on, got the boarding passes in my hand in Zurich to distribute them to our people. But I had no real idea what these passes were good for. Until then I had only flown on domestic flights and did not know anything about seat reservations for international flights. When I boarded the plane, I still had some of these passes in my hand. That was idiotic, of course. A stewardess raced after me and took them off me when I was already on the plane. She obviously thought I was stupid, and I was.

It finally turned out that three seats remained empty. Three of our top ladies had not come. I wasn't surprised about something like that anymore. Obviously, Maharishi had held them back at the very last minute.

In Paris we had a stay of many hours. And instead of requesting the boarding passes for the intercontinental flight immediately after our Paris arrival, which would have allowed me to choose good seats in the non-smoking area, I waited until shortly before departure. I was very inexperienced. As a result, I then had great difficulty in calming down our demanding ladies or rearranging the seating, because many of us had to sit in the smoking area. Finally, the plane took off for India.

The three missing ladies joined us at the very last second. They had followed in the private jet and were now flying first class. I myself, like others, sat in the middle of the smoking section of Economy Class. Nevertheless, I enjoyed the flight. Finally, I could relax! I got myself seated, and listened to Chopin almost the whole flight via the on-board equipment and even had time to doze and dream. Arriving at Delhi airport, we took a rickety, crooked and dirty bus through the dry and dusty country to the city. The early morning sun shone on groves of exotic trees, under which elephants walked. Everything was still quiet and fresh. Happiness was in the air, although I felt a little uneasy inside. It was my first encounter with a totally alien world. We unloaded the luggage in front of the Lodhi Hotel. Surprisingly, almost all the suitcases were found after some searching. Only Maharishi's cook Mohan missed his: 'Suitcase Mohan no.'

There was not much to do in the first few days. An Indian woman, Kirti, a top lady in Maharishi's staff, and, as insiders knew, his niece, gave us instructions on how best to stay healthy: 'No unwashed fruit; preferably only eat cooked food; in the restaurant, no water, but only drink Coca Cola or soft drinks, and that only if the lid is still sealed, otherwise it could be 'diluted'.

I still remember the first yogic flying sessions, outside in the garden of the hotel. We enjoyed the Flying Sutra in tents, where a wide-open space between wall and roof was left free for air circulation. Absolutely necessary in this heat! Through these spaces, one could look up to the sky. Vultures circled above us in hazy light. Of course, we did not 'fly' on foam mattresses, which did not exist in India, but on dusty cotton mats, which were stacked in several layers on top of each other. Landing was always quite hard.

But everywhere there was bliss, bliss, bliss. Happiness was simply in the air. Nevertheless, after the some time, I preferred to do my 'program' in the room, where in the beginning cooled air came out of a shaft and later, almost without a transition, hot air. I soon appreciated the latter, because in winter, it can get quite cold in Delhi.

After one or two weeks of acclimatization and lazing around, suddenly instructions from Maharishi came. It was only now that I realized that a large Course had been scheduled in Delhi with about 3,000 participants from all over the world. Topic: Vedic Science. Our group was to meet the arrivals at the airport and distribute them to their respective widely scattered hotels in Delhi. For many days. flights with course participants arrived from all over the world, almost always early in the morning. In front of or behind the official control desks at the airport we had set up our own stands where we registered the arrivals and sent them to their respective buses.

Maharishi had taken care of many details. For example, he wanted all buses to have numbers, and these numbers we were to be handed out to the arriving participants, depending on the hotel destination. Unfortunately, I took this instruction a bit lightly, especially since groups and individual travelers kept arriving about whom we had not been informed, so we often had to improvise and use buses differently than planned. We spent whole days and partly nights at the airport. Again, there was very little sleep. One morning, after a long and exhausting night, I was still hanging around in a sweat, when someone drew my attention to the personal Indian 'boy' and driver of Maharishi, who was also in the 'Arrivals' area. Should Maharishi himself be arriving today? We grabbed the boy. Yes, indeed, Maharishi was expected in a few hours. I quickly organized a taxi, drove to the hotel, washed myself, changed clothes, bought a garland of flowers from a street vendor on the way back, and then waited again at the airport.

Finally, Maharishi's plane arrived. Together with Indian supporters we organized the arrival so that he didn't have to go through the normal passport control, but could use the back entrance as a VIP. There I waited for him, almost alone, and welcomed him. I tried to put my somewhat modest, not quite fresh and unfortunately not homemade flower garland over his head. But Maharishi held his hand over his head and did not let me, despite a second attempt. It was a little embarrassing for me. And of course, I thought about what I might have done wrong, and whether he was angry with me.

Maharishi then went through an area where I was not allowed to follow him, and after some time his car came out on the other side of the building, where I had already hurried. He drove past me in some distance. Then the car stopped, the window rolled down, and Maharishi beckoned me: 'Do you know where I will be staying?' I made a guess, which was wrong. Nandkishore, who accompanied him, said, 'Indian Express Building – the building of the famous Indian Express newspaper.' Maharishi said, 'Come there,' and the car drove off.

I immediately got into one of the rickety and dirty auto rickshaws. Rarely in my life have I been so happy as in the half hour of this trip: Maharishi had invited me specially! He wanted my report! He was obviously not upset about my clumsy attempt with the garland! I enjoyed the bliss that was hanging in the air even in the ugly streets of New Delhi. At the same time, I was naturally excited about what Maharishi would probably say to me. The taxi driver finally found the building which was still under construction. I went to the entrance, which was not guarded. Only in front of the inner door stood a guard. I said, 'I am Maharishi's secretary; he wants to see me.' The man did not know Maharishi at all, only his own boss Mr. Goenka. But impressed by my resolute appearance he let me in. I entered the suite that was actually Goenka's private suite, which he had made available to Maharishi for that time. It was a completely new section of the Indian Express building, but of course, I didn't know that yet.

In the living and meeting room sat only Maharishi, Goenka, Nandkishore, and Praveen, a nephew of Maharishi, as he was unofficially known. I sat down and gave my report. Promptly Maharishi also asked for about numbers on the buses. It became clear that I had not followed the instructions exactly. Maharishi raised his eyebrows. Fortunately, Praveen came to my aid. As Hans has said, many groups arrived without previous notification and we had to revise the system again and again.

Maharishi seemed satisfied, but I felt a little uncomfortable. In the days that followed, I still didn't know what to expect about what, would be my task and my status here in India,. I had not yet been deeply involved in the whole project. Not even Maharishi's arrival had been announced to me.

After a day or two, I was given more clarity. The great festival of light, Dipavali was being celebrated. That corresponds roughly to Christmas in our country. All 3,000 students were to come to Noida, a development area outside Delhi, where our Movement had bought a large desert-like piece of land. There the celebration was to take place in a huge tent, in the presence of the Shankaracharya (the equivalent of 'Pope' to the Hindus)! I was given the task of inviting the course participants, who were scattered far and wide in Delhi, and possibly organizing their transport. This was really not an easy task on India's biggest holiday, where hardly any bus company or taxi driver was willing to work! Besides, the Indian telephone system at that time was not as good as the German one. Just reaching the reception of the hotel and asking for a connection was more difficult than if we wanted to call Papua New Guinea today, and the connection was often worse. Most of the time you could only make yourself understood by shouting into the receiver.

We staff members tried, on all available telephones to contact the participants in the different hotels and shout the message through them. As we could only organize a few buses, they generally had to solve the question of transport themselves. All we had to do was explain the location and time to them. As if by a miracle, everyone arrived in Noida in the evening. I sat down on a mat in the audience area. Little by little, the participants arrived. In the middle of the huge tent hall sat hundreds of Indian pandit students,[*19] mostly boys, and followers of the Shankaracharya. Directly in front of them, under the wide stage, stood large, flat baskets of piled up Indian sweets: Ladhus, burfi, fruits etc. There were also stacks of golden yellow cotton scarves as gifts of the TM-movement for the pandit boys.

After a long wait, the Shankaracharya finally came in with his entourage and settled on his throne. Behind him, Maharishi climbed onto the stage and sat down on a flat, much lower seat at the feet of the Shankaracharya.

The celebration consisted mainly of a long puja in honor of Mahalakshmi.[*20] Many pandits in beautiful red robes performed Vedic recitations to propitiate Mahalakshmi and to obtain grace. This was apparently successful, as an enormously powerful atmosphere was created. After the Puja and the following Bhajans,[*21] where all Indians who were present joined, an unpleasant scene took place. When it came to the distribution of the 'sweets' that were offered in the Puja, the young pandit disciples stormed forward and raided them so greedily that the helpers of the Shankaracharya had to beat them brutally with ropes to push them back. Otherwise they would have trampled down all the sweets in the midst of which they stood while they stuffed them into their mouths. As a result, the crowd swayed back and forth, as the ones in front retreated because they received the blows of the guards, but from behind, more and more boys were pushing in. The Shankaracharya and Maharishi watched with very unhappy faces.

When the ceremony was over, many Westerners and Indians, crowded around the Shankaracharya and Maharishi on the spacious stage. Then the Shankaracharya discreetly left. I viewed him as a kind and wise man, as a special human being, but not in the same class as Maharishi, who I thought was a fully enlightened Master.

Soon the stage was full of people. I thought, 'Why shouldn't I go up there, too? Maybe I could get close to Maharishi.' No sooner said than done. I climbed onto the podium, pushed and shoved myself inconspicuously into Maharishi's vicinity and enjoyed his charisma. After some time, Maharishi gave a sign that everyone should leave. Nandkishore, who had seen me, called me and told me to go to the microphone and ask all participants, mainly the Westerners, again and again to leave the tent and go home. In a calm voice, I repeated the same words repeatedly. Everyone should please leave now. Gradually the students pushed their way to the exits. Maharishi would be the last to leave the tent.

Finally, only a few very close staff members, mostly Indians, were left on the stage with Maharishi, who spoke to them in a very relaxed manner. When he left, he gave me the order to check if all participants had found a transport possibility. He would wait for me in his car, and then we would leave at the same time. I scurried around the grounds and was finally able to report that everyone was gone. On the drive back, in the last car, close behind Maharishi, I was again totally reveling in my luck. I knew: I am still 'in'. I will also have a job here in India and will be 'secretary'. Indeed, in the following days it turned out that I was responsible for all matters that were somehow connected with the Course and that concerned the Westerners. For Indian affairs, there were Indian secretaries.

Now I have to tell you something about the location of the Course. It was indeed unusual. As I said, it was a newly constructed building that was still unfinished and had been attached at an angle to the old Indian Express building. As I later found out, Mr. Goenka had started the new building without permission and was then stopped by the authorities so that he was not allowed to furnish and use it. He then made it available to us.

There was a wedge-shaped narrow gap between the two wings of buildings. Here, covered by a tarpaulin, the kitchen for our Course had been set up. Many Indian workers squatted there all day long, chopping vegetables, sizzling and frying.

Both buildings were four stories high. In the old building, the activity of the newspaper was continued, and on the ground floor, Maharishi lived in Goenka's personal suite. The new wing housed the dining room, the lecture hall, the two 'flying' rooms one for men and one for women and, on the top floor, very importantly, the clinic. The latter, like all other rooms, consisted of a huge hall. In one corner, separated by tarpaulins, the doctors had set up the department for the seriously ill cases, equipped with camp beds. The larger part, however, was covered with cotton mats on which people with flu and diarrhea, for example, could lie down. They could follow the lectures that took place downstairs on the first floor via video monitors. It was practically always crowded during the first weeks of the Course. I, too, caught a bad flu soon after the beginning and lay on a mat for several days among all the other coughing and sniffling people.

The hall on the ground floor became the dining hall. Under the tables at the edge, on which mostly mountains of fruit were spread out, one could hear the Indian workers, cleaners and other helpers, snoring late in the evening, because that was where they slept. The two wings of the big building met in a corner. There they had built a temporary crossing on the first floor. Since the height of the two buildings was different, a few steps had to be built. They consisted of somewhat wobbly, leather upholstered old furniture parts. On them Maharishi had to climb from the old part of the building to the large lecture hall.

This once resulted in a small happy experience for me. It was at the end of a long lecture in front of the entire group of course participants. As usual, I walked behind the Master when he left; as his secretary, I enjoyed this privilege. As usual, I had in my hand any files or documents I was working on. As usual, I walked diagonally to the left behind Maharishi to the back exit of the hall and had my portfolio in my left hand. Then I had the idea to take the books in my right hand so that I could support the master with my left hand in case he should stumble on the shaky steps.

Was it intuition or did Maharishi do me a favor? He actually lost his balance on the stairs, threw up his left arm and tumbled to the left. As quick as lightning, I grabbed him by the arm with my left hand, unfortunately a bit violently, so that it clamped properly, and straightened him up again.

Maharishi went on calmly. I, glowing with pride, followed him; and this time I felt entitled to get into the elevator with him, which I generally avoided, so as not to bother him with my overexcited state and body odor, because most of the time I was quite sweaty from the Indian heat and all the rushing around. Maharishi of course noticed my pride and smiled at me. I was just a bit embarrassed that I had grabbed him so hard; I still felt the impact on my hand.

The Vedic Science Course was officially scheduled to last only one month. But when that month was up, course activities were continuing. Maharishi invited the people to stay. Many did so, for months; some applied for international staff; and I had the task of presenting their application forms to Maharishi, listening to his comments, and sometimes forwarding them.

For example, it turned out that he never accepted bi-national couples. He was even more adverse to mixed-race couples. Twice, someone came to me who wanted to be Maharishi's personal secretary. Although I had not the slightest interest in having someone else next to me or even having someone replace me, I felt, as mentioned before, that I had to tell Maharishi. In both cases, Maharishi wanted to see the people, and one of them was given certain duties.

I hardly followed the knowledge aspect of the Course, although I was able to attend the lectures frequently and always had a good seat, right next to the stage. But I did not recall much, because my head was always full of all kinds of things I had to do and organize. And that was a lot. There were several thousand course participants staying in about 75 Delhi hotels and guest houses, and all needed to be bussed back and forth each day. I also had to handle all the international mail.

Here, too, I was constantly carrying all the letters around in my little suitcase. Often, I was squatting on the floor, the employees of Goenka and Maharishi's Indian secretaries running around me, in the corridor in front of the door to his suite. Apart from me, no Westerners were allowed in this corridor; it was Goenka's private wing and was guarded by his people. I spread the mail out on the floor and made marginal notes. Then everything went to the 'secretaries' of the individual countries, who then wrote the answers. The intercom to Maharishi was close by, and often I had to quickly get everything together and stuff it into the suitcase when Maharishi called to give me an assignment. If I were under too much pressure because of too much mail, I would hide in the meeting room when it was unused. It was also in this wing. There was a narrow space between the wall and the curtain where I could concentrate better, of course, not without having told an Indian secretary where to find me.

As soon as I came out of this corridor into the public area, there were generally some westerners crowding around me who wanted to discuss something with Maharishi. Often, I also had to approve money from the cash box, which I had to manage. On the one hand, this harassment of 'petitioners' was extremely stressful, because I always had to concentrate fully to get a comprehensive impression of the respective story as quickly as possible. On the other hand, I was happy about everyone who came to me, because maybe he gave me another reason to contact Maharishi.

Sometimes I went to the huge 'flying' room' in the basement of the building for the flying program. Its ceiling was very high, thank God, because with hundreds of sweating 'hoppers' the air was not the freshest. I hid in a corner. The lighting was not too bright. Nevertheless, I could almost be sure that inevitably an Indian Secretary would come down the stairs and call for me because Maharishi wanted something from me. I quickly got dressed again, happy and excited that Maharishi had called for me and at the same time proud because everyone heard that I was wanted by him. Maharishi pushed me to the limit of my endurance. I could survive only if I let go of myself completely.

My living situation also contributed to my 'softening'. Eventually, we staff members from the Lodhi Hotel had to move to less expensive accommodations. I came to the hotel 'Marina' that was centrally located on Connaught Circus in the heart of the business district of downtown Delhi. This was a hotel with few amenities, without air conditioning, with bare stone walls and the same kind of floor. I was quite lucky in that I got a room that had windows on both sides. Then, in March, when the hot weather started, I could lie in the cross draft at nights and that helped to cool me down a little.

But unfortunately, right under my window there was a main crossing with traffic lights, on which there was total chaos from approximately 5:00 AM onward. Not only that, every few minutes the crowd started with exhaust fumes and noise, there was also the typical vehicle horns honking, which practically never stopped. In India, one is not perceived as a road user if one does not use the horn all the time. I could not close the window because of the heat. So my sleep was disturbed quite early in the morning, to put it mildly. But I continued dozing, because I was simply too exhausted.

Usually I had only returned from the Indian Express at midnight the night before, through a hot night air of about 35 degrees Celsius. To walk all the way back on foot was too far; I had to take a taxi. But that was not easy at this time, although there was a tent directly in front of the 'Indian Express building, where about 10 taxi drivers slept. There was even a telephone in it, with the usual miserable connection, where one hardly understood a word. And the taxi drivers typically did not speak English anyway. I called from the building, but if someone answered the phone after a long time of ringing, I only got an incomprehensible grunt, whereupon they hung up again. I often went directly to the tent and tried to wake someone up, but mostly everybody wanted to continue sleeping. Then I had to walk to the next bigger place to stop a taxi that happened to pass by. A few times, I actually preferred to walk another hour to the hotel.

Meanwhile the burden of the work lay mostly on my shoulders, because Wolfgang, who had arrived in India together with Maharishi, gradually withdrew more and more. Not only he could not stand the heat, but he also wanted to enjoy life instead of getting so tired. He lived in a hotel with air conditioning. After I once spent a meditation in his cool room, I had the courage to ask Maharishi for an air-conditioned room, but he refused. Wolfgang was not a selfless type like me, who liked to take privations. On the other hand, I was always there, waiting in front of the suite near the intercom, and therefore received Maharishi's orders, the outcome of which I was then able to report on again. Thus, I gradually became the main secretary for 'Western' affairs.

Already on January 8th, when Maharishi came out of his annual 'Silence', he called me in as the first of all Westerners. This was a special honor and also a special happiness for me. Maharishi's charisma after seven days of seclusion and fasting was simply incredible: so subtle, so loving, so physically fragile and yet so powerful.

I went into the suite, in which besides Maharishi only Nandkishore and Goenka were sitting. He spoke a few sentences with me and then instructed me to call in all the other leading Westerners: among them Wolfgang, former secretaries like Neil P. and John C., Geoffrey C., the main Course leader under Maharishi, and some others. This recognition was one of the highlights of my 'career'.

Another highlight had happened shortly before the India trip. I had been commissioned by Maharishi to give the last secret instructions to the participants of the TTC (teacher training course), which was just finishing. Actually, I had only inserted the most secret audio tape and started the recorder. But I felt that at that moment I was radiating a huge aura of power and light, an expression of the authority I had borrowed from Maharishi.

By the way, Maharishi had tested me for my trustworthiness some time before. When he gave the final instructions for another TTC, I was the one who had to thoroughly check the room and its surroundings to make sure that nobody was in or near it. I myself stayed in the hall as the only non-participant, but I hid myself in the back corner of the room, near one of the big glass doors and rustled with the curtain, so that I could not hear anything. The Master spoke to the people through a headphone system. When he had left the room and I cleaned it up, I noticed a paper on his table that he had left there.

I guessed immediately that these were his reminders for the most secret instructions. I conscientiously avoided looking at them, folded the paper together and put it in my pocket. Later, I showed him the folded paper in his meeting room and asked what I should do with it. He said, very cool and without showing any emotion, 'Tear it up,' which I then did carefully in his presence. I am sure this was a test. If I had not passed it, he would certainly not have entrusted me with the secret audio tape.

But I did not pass all the tests and when I did not, I always felt it immediately. Once Maharishi was expecting a very special guest in India, but at the same time he wanted to hold the course lecture in the great hall, and he gave me the order to inform him as soon as the guest arrived. I lurked around at the entrance, and I was sorry that I could not be at the lecture and near him. Finally, I asked a very trustworthy person, one of the veteran and leading American staff members, who was working in the entrance area anyway, to inform me immediately when this guest arrived, and went to the hall.

When Maharishi realized that I was not at my post, he quietly instructed an Indian secretary to go to the entrance. It was then very painful for me when after some time this secretary came into the hall and gave Maharishi a sign that the guest was there, whereupon Maharishi immediately stopped the lecture and went out to receive him. This was the kind of education Maharishi gave me. He never said a word about the incident afterwards.

At the end of the one-month course, the participants began to return home group by group. As always, Maharishi wanted to see all departing participants in person just before their flight. I was responsible for organizing the meetings and transportation to the airport. The planes usually took off after midnight. Every evening a group of between 20 to 70 people waited in Maharishi's meeting room to receive the final blessing. I had calculated exactly when the bus or buses had to leave in order to get to the airport on time. Most of the time, I had also arranged for luggage to be transported there in advance so that it could be checked in and the plane would not leave without our people. Maharishi was informed about the time of departure. But in spite of it all, he arrived at the room at about the time when the participants should have left, as expected. He spoke to all, completely calm, answered questions and addressed special concerns.

The participants were mostly quite relaxed due to their stay in India and the presence of Maharishi. They knew that everything would go well. I should have known it too, but the further the departure time was exceeded, the more restless I became. From time to time, I gave Maharishi a sign: Now people really have to go! But he remained calm. I literally stood in the door with my hands wringing. Several airlines had already told me: 'If your people are late again, we'll just fly off and never take passengers from your organization again.'

Then, from one minute to the next, Maharishi said, 'Now you must go.' And now it was important that everyone left immediately, because Maharishi had a good sense of how far he could go. I seem to recall that one time a flight was actually missed, and that was because some of the participants were eager to discuss personal matters with Maharishi, even though he was urging them to leave.

One of these farewell-meetings is especially memorable to me: The people leaving were almost exclusively Americans. Maharishi spoke about the evil methods of the American government to start wars all over the world in order to supply both sides with weapons. He called the USA 'the most criminal country of the world', also in reference to the high crime rate in the USA. Then he said, 'It's just bad luck to be born in America.' The course participants were naturally shocked and shaken. Some asked, 'What should we do? Should we emigrate?' Maharishi said, 'No,' and repeated several times his sentence, 'It is simply a misfortune to be born in America.' This was, in contrast to other sessions, a very depressing farewell for the participants.

At the end of these meetings, some students usually had certain things blessed by Maharishi, such as Rudraksha malas[*22] and the like. Once someone brought a beautiful Shiva-Lingam[*23] weighing several kilograms and placed it in front of Maharishi. Maharishi was delighted with the beautiful specimen and then said, 'Leave it with me. You will get it later.' The man was apparently an advanced devotee, for he agreed to part with the lingam without batting an eyelid. He probably knew, like me, that he would never see his lingam again. The reason why Maharishi wanted to keep the lingam was probably, apart from the export ban of the Indian government, that according to the Vedic lore, one should possess three-dimensional representations of the deities only if one worships them every day with a prescribed puja. But this can only be done by a trained pundit and by no means by a Westerner.

The heat became more and more intense from the end of February onwards, but I began to enjoy it. The power of the sun almost kills you. When I traveled in the open scooter dressed only with thin Kurta[*24] and Dhoti[*5] through the streets and the hot air blew around the body, I was totally in bliss, a bliss, which one can find only in India. Here you had to give up any self-will, actually any planning, because such a thing would have been too exhausting. I had to learn to let go completely and to let myself drift with Nature. Finally, it got up to 45° C. The air was like a hot wall. Once I had to drive in a car with a group of young Indians crowded together. We left the windows closed, very different from what you would do in a similar situation in the West. Because the heat coming in from outside was much more than the heat inside the car, because every sweating body, even with its 37° C, contributed to the cooling!

One fine day there was a first small sign that my wonderful time was coming to an end. It was already April. A new course had been announced for Western participants. It should take place in Kashmir. Maharishi called Wolfgang and me on the intercom and said that one of us should go to Kashmir to check it out. We should decide among ourselves who would go. It was clear that none of us wanted to leave Maharishi. I said, 'Maybe Wolfgang should go, because he's more experienced at negotiating.' Maharishi replied, 'The negotiations have been concluded.' Then I realized that Maharishi intended to make me leave. So, I said, 'I am going.' Maharishi was satisfied.

In Kashmir there was actually not much to do for me. There were still a few small things to prepare for the course; but that was done by Sushil and the beautiful Anjou, a young Indian couple from the area. The Course was to take place at and on Lake Dal, the tourist attraction in

Srinagar. The lake was situated in an open high valley with the snowy Himalayan Mountains in the background. The participants would live on picturesque and richly decorated wooden houseboats. Actually, in spite of the wonderful scenery, I had the impression, 'What's the point?' I preferred the noisy and polluted city of New Delhi. Even in that hot stone desert I still felt the Indian spirituality and the underlying bliss. I missed that in Kashmir.

At first, I lived in a hotel near the lake, but then I moved to a small island whose surface was almost completely filled with a big house. The island was only about 30 meters away from the shore. But one had to cross over with a boat. This was the home of the enterprising Kuru brothers, our local partners who coordinated most of the lake's houseboats and ran a kind of travel agency. In their house, I got a room on the first floor. They assured me that the water in this house came through a pipe from the municipal waterworks, so it was clean. This was quite a contrast to the water for washing and showering on the houseboats, which was pumped directly from the lake, a filter made of linen cloth holding back the raw sewage that ran into the lake.

So, I risked brushing my teeth with the water that came out of my tap. What I didn't know was that the water in my room, in distinction from the others, came from the lake. Later I discovered the small water tank on a pole near the shore in front of my window, into which the lake water was pumped and then led through a fabric filter to my tap.

Soon the students arrived. I gave a short speech to them only once, otherwise we did not have much to do with each other. I could sightsee around the area for endless days.

Then came the fatal day, which signalled the beginning of my 'fall'. In the morning, I received the indirect message from Maharishi via the telephone of the Kuru brothers that I should return to Delhi immediately. I was relieved and happy to finally be allowed to go back to him. I thought, 'Now let's just get out of here quickly, so that I don't get any contrary news, in case Maharishi should have decided otherwise in the meantime.'

A really stupid thought! Maybe this was one of the deeper reasons why I was haunted by bad luck from that moment on, although I had bathed in constant 'support by nature' until then. I thought about that for a long time afterwards.

First, I gave the travel agent of the Kurus the order to organize a flight for me, for today and immediately! In the meantime, I quickly packed my travel bag. I did not even take the time to organize cash. The taxi was ready, and I left at the last minute to catch the flight. Unfortunately, the driver had to fill up the tank, which cost valuable time; and he apparently could not drive very fast with his vehicle. But I was pretty sure of my 'support'. Probably the departure would be delayed somehow, so that I could still fly. But when I arrived at the airport, I saw the plane rolling out onto the runway. There was nothing more to be done, not even with my arrival.

Should I now drive back to the room I had already vacated, which was perhaps already occupied by someone else? How would it look like as I had said goodbye after that 'triumphant' farewell – Maharishi having called me personally! – 'beaten back? No! There must be another possibility.' And indeed, it turned out that the same day a plane would fly to Jammu, at least in the direction of Delhi. And there was supposed to be a connecting flight to Delhi, but they could not tell from there whether there were any seats left on it. I risked it, as I was used to having 'support of nature', especially since I was working for Maharishi. Probably it was only a cosmic test of trust, I thought. So, I had my ticket rewritten.

The flight over the Himalaya peaks was wonderful. I sat on a window seat in an almost empty plane and looked down on snow-covered mountains, river valleys and small villages. A certain anxiety remained, but gradually I relaxed. The airport of Jammu was far outside the village and consisted only of a runway and a small bare concrete building with a waiting room, an office and a counter, no bigger than a village train station. I waited for the plane to Delhi. When it arrived, tiny, some people got off and others got on.

And then it turned out that not a single seat was free for me. Boom! It hit me like a hammer. Had the cosmos stopped taking care of me? Had my wrong thought been so bad that I was now punished by Nature? Had I fallen from grace? I was not used to such things. I got into a slight panic, lost my inner strength, which I had always had despite hectic work. What should I do now? The next plane would not take off until tomorrow. Now it was afternoon. Should I sleep here in this desolate station on the bench? I did not even have cash for the taxi to Jammu city and a hotel room. The airport manager suggested I could get a refund for the flight to Delhi and then take the train from Jammu. Excited as I was, I could hardly think a calm and clear thought. Finally, I said, 'Yes, please pay me the money.' From that, I thought I could at least afford a first-class night train with air conditioning. I got into one of the taxis that were available and drove towards the city.

On the way, confused as I was, I began to doubt again, 'Shouldn't I take the flight tomorrow after all?' I had the taxi driver turn around. But shortly before the airport, I decided differently, 'No, but please go to the train station.' Arriving there, I found huge queues at all counters; it seemed I had to stand in line for hours, another shock. Finally, I was guided to a special counter. The Indians often still treated Western foreigners like a Master race. This was almost embarrassing for me, but in this case, it was of course useful. It turned out that there were no more first-class seats available on both night trains that would still be going to Delhi today. Another shock! I imagined how I had to spend the 18 hours in a wagon packed with sweating locals. I had seen how crowded the Indian trains in general were in the lower price ranges while waiting at the gates. It was not uncommon for people to hang around outside the car or sit on the roof of the train wagon. But I was told that on one of the two trains, the later one, a second-class berth was still available, but without air conditioning. I had to take that one.

Until departure, there were still a few hours left, which I spent in the evening sun on a station bench, shoving my travel bag under my head, so that it could not be stolen. After some time, I started to enjoy the scenery around me again. In particular I observed two impressive Swamis[*25] with long, knotted hair and white beard. They obviously had their possessions with them in a cloth roll. But when they started smoking, I was a bit disillusioned; and even more when I saw how excited they were running back and forth when the train arrived.

Then came the time when the first of the two Delhi trains were to depart, the one for which no seat ticket had been available. I went to the appropriate platform and looked to see if the situation might have changed. An Indian railway official advised me to simply get on this train and wait there in the vestibule of the first-class car to see if there was a seat available. That would happen frequently. Again, I took the risk. I got on and stood, still a little indecisive, next to the door. The train started. I waited a long time for the conductor to get through with this wagon. And again, there was not a single seat left. I had to get off at the next station, after about two hours of travel, and wait there for 'my' train.

This station was literally 'in the middle of nowhere'. There was no station building, not even a real platform, and no one in sight. In the meantime, it had already become pitch-dark. I laid down on one of the benches and looked up into the sky. Seldom have I seen such a wonderfully clear starry sky. This was apparently a very, very sparsely populated area, actually a kind of desert. A village lay a little apart. No 'light pollution' except a station lantern in the distance. There was almost no sound, just silence. Imagine that something like that still existed! Only in the far distance, I could hear a dog barking from time to time. It was absolutely blissful, and I began to enjoy it. If only the worry and the anxiety about reaching my destination had not been in the back of my mind.

After two hours, I heard my train approaching in the distance. When it finally, stopped, with squeaking brakes, I already doubted my chances of embarking by now. I rushed along the train, in order to find my wagon with the reserved seat. Of course, it was at the far end. Hopefully the train would not leave without me! Finally, I saw my car number. I wanted to open the door, but it was locked! And there was no one around. In my panic, I banged on the door for a long time. Finally, someone came and opened it for me from inside. Phew!

As soon as I got on the train, it started to move, but where was my place now? In the half-light, I somehow found it. Of course, someone was already lying there. Fortunately, Indian people are usually very authority-conscious, and so the man immediately made my place free and squeezed himself in with his family. The conductor came. Everything is fine. I relaxed a little. My wooden bench was, unusually, lengthwise in the direction of the train, under an open, as usual barred, window. I hung my light jacket, with passport and everything in it, over me, pushed my bag under the bench and lay down. From my seat I could now look up into the sky again; the warm night air blew around me. I surrendered to the present and enjoyed it. Now and then, we stopped at a small station where people slept like sardines, side by side on the platform. They did not let the train disturb them. The sleepy voice of the announcers, the rattling train, the Indian scent, the stars, everything again was total bliss! I fell asleep. A few times, I woke up and each time I saw an Indian police officer in a brown uniform with a rifle, who apparently guarded our car in particular, leaning against the wall near me. At six o' clock, it was already light, I bought a soft drink at a station, pulled my bag out from under me and fiddled around in it; the policeman was still there. I lay down again and fell asleep again.

At 8 o' clock, I woke up again, wanted to get something out of my bag and could not find it anymore. But that could not be! I looked around the whole compartment – nothing! Could someone have stolen it? My unimposing Indian travelling bag? The policeman was 'unfortunately' no longer there. I ran out onto the platform, but saw no policeman anywhere. I thought, 'If someone stole the bag, he might take out the 'valuable' things right away, my electric razor, my travel alarm clock and my little binoculars, and leave the bag somewhere.' For me, actually only the Ayurvedic liver pills were important, which Dr. Dwivedi, the famous Indian Vaidya[*27] and herbal specialist, had produced especially for us western course participants for prevention of liver problems. So, I searched the station, always worried that the train might leave without me. Then I found the policeman, spoke to him; but he did not understand English. The bag could not be found. I got back on as the train was leaving.

Around noon, we finally arrived in Delhi. I reported my theft at the station and went to the 'Indian Express'. Totally sweaty and dusty I immediately went to Maharishi's Intercom and called him. He said, 'I'm glad you're here; I already asked where you were.' I told him what had gone wrong and that I had had so little 'nature support' that I thought he did not want me to come at all. 'No, no,' he said. 'I wanted you to come and report back to me.' After a brief pause, he added, 'And fly back again today.' I was shocked. I wanted to rest, at least wash up. In addition, I had to get a new bag and all the other traveling clothes. But of course, I was not going to argue. Fortunately, I found people who bought everything I needed in a few hours at the nearby Chandni Chowk market. In the evening, I was already sitting in the plane going to Kashmir again.

In the following weeks, I flew back and forth between Kashmir and Delhi several times. In Kashmir, I lived now on a houseboat. I took part in negotiations with other boat owners, because in the meantime a second phase of the Course started with many more participants. I noticed that the first boats were expensive. The Kuru brothers, who had been given the job, had probably thought more about their commission than about our interests. Although I was not a businessperson, I negotiated much lower prices for better boats.

But apart from that, I still did not have much to do. Finally, the Course ended and I returned to Delhi for good. There everything seemed strange to me. There was only a relatively small group left, maybe about a hundred of our staff, old and new ones; the 'flying' area was now somewhere else. Maharishi hardly ever appeared, but gave the impression that he wanted to stay in India permanently.

He sent many of our people on tour in teams of two to introduce people to TM throughout the country. In doing so, he wanted to take advantage of the fact that the daily newspaper 'Indian Express' had repeatedly reported about the Course, sometimes with full-page in-depth descriptions of the 'Vedic Science'. One day he called my friend Jürgen Zander, a hypermotivated and, in my opinion, highly developed enlightenment seeker, India fan and already almost Hindu, together with me to the intercom and asked us to travel through India together, to give presentations and to spread the word about TM. Jürgen was enthusiastic; I on the other hand was sad.

Now we needed new visas, because our old ones could not be extended, after eight months. We decided to fly to Nepal to apply for new entry visas at the Indian Embassy a few weeks later. So we hung around in Kathmandu for some time, visiting temples and sight-seeing. When we finally thought we could go to the office without fear of arousing suspicion, we realized that it was not so easy to get a new visa. At first, we were rejected and had to think of something new.

Then something happened that threw all my plans, even my whole future perspective, into a tail-spin. When I woke up after an afternoon nap, I felt extremely dull. This haze in my head did not go away. The next day I felt more and more like I had fallen out of the world, miserable and sick in a very severe way. The next day I decided to see a doctor, of course an Ayurvedic one; for that was what Maharishi would have recommended.

It was as if the cosmos had done everything possible to sicken me, starting with using bad water in Kashmir, followed by the theft of the liver pills, and then the distance from Maharishi. Now, to make matters worse, I also was examined by a very unexperienced Vaidya,[*27] a young, absolute beginner, who was being instructed by an older one sitting next to him. The young man prescribed a remedy against fever and one against diarrhea.

As it turned out soon afterwards, I suffered from amoebic dysentery and jaundice at the same time. I got worse and worse every day. Finally, Jürgen took me to a western doctor. This one recognized the hepatitis immediately and prescribed me a cortisone preparation. At that time, I had no idea about these things and did not resist. But unfortunately, cortisone only lowers the fever, and thus suspends the natural healing process. In fact, my body temperature dropped. My skin became more and more yellow, finally orange. Even in my mouth, I was bright yellow, my urine dark yellow-brown. I was now lying in a single room of our modest hotel; Jürgen seldom came by, as he had to deal with his visa business. Finally, he travelled back to Delhi. An American TM teacher, who was staying in the same hotel, provided me with food. I was almost always alone and suffered terribly. I always had fever, even if only mild, a constant misery and some kind of nausea, and more and more and more fear, more anxiety and anxiety and fear. From the house next door, which was only two feet from one of my windows, ghastly food smells were coming through. I was getting weaker and weaker.

Nevertheless, in the hope that this would make me healthy, I tried to keep up my meditation program. To 'fly' I would pull my mattress to the floor with some effort each time. But this effort was not good for me at all. I did practically everything wrong: the medicine, the meditation practice, the effort of flying… Finally, our German doctor, Uli Bauhofer, called me from Delhi or from Switzerland, on behalf of Maharishi. I dragged myself to the reception of the hotel and talked to him. My voice was already very weak. Uli advised me to stop taking the cortisone. He also said that Maharishi had returned to Switzerland. That hit me like a blow. I had so fervently hoped to get back to him quickly; and now he was not even in India! This separation was actually the worst thing.

For weeks and months on end, I checked every day whether I was feeling better and whether I could go back to him. I felt such impatience and longing! It was as if the closest, long-time lover had left me. And so it was in a way. On top of that, my whole purpose in life, my status in the community, and everything in general had been connected with Maharishi and my job as secretary. I had lost everything that had been dear and important to me. It was cruel.

I vegetated for a more few weeks. Finally, Dr. Eberhard B., a German doctor and member of our group, took me back to Switzerland on an endlessly exhausting journcy. To my disappointment, I was not taken to the 'Capital' where Maharishi lived, but to a nearby hospital. I understood that quarantine was necessary because of the danger of infection. In the hospital, I was given a single room with a beautiful view of a mountain range illuminated by the autumn sun, from whose height the hang-gliders often took off. I could actually have had a good time: no responsibility, and no stress. I was well taken care of, everything was pleasant, bright and clean. The weather was mostly sunny, a wonderful autumn. But the vague fear that something terrible was going on and that I would never regain my strength prevented me from relaxing. And the impatience! When would I ever come back to Maharishi? I still checked from day to day whether my condition was improving. It was not.

Maharishi had made sure that I received all the audio tapes I wanted. Every night I listened to the lessons of the second part of the TTC, the teacher-training course. It was wonderful knowledge of the deepest laws of Being. Maharishi seemed like an intellectual giant. How could anyone have such deep insights! I listened to the tapes all night long because I could hardly sleep due to constant and heavy itching of the skin, a side effect of hepatitis. After many weeks without progress, the chief physician decided that I should have another dose of cortisone. Now it made some sense, because it could stifle the chronic fever. Finally, I was found stable enough to leave the hospital. My mother picked me up. She happened to be nearby and brought me to her home in Reinbek.

After some weeks, I asked Maharishi if I could return to Seelisberg. He allowed it. Also, here I still lay in bed most of the time. Maharishi had just been away. When he came back one day, I waited for him, weak as I was, in front of his suite. When he went in, the security man would not let me through because I was no longer a secretary. But I just managed to squeeze through the door behind Maharishi. I sat with him in his meeting room while he had the secretary's report to him via intercom.

Finally, he turned to me. I told him about the homeopathic remedies that I had been prescribed by a doctor in Hamburg. 'We don't know the system', he expressed with skepticism. But after some back and forth he suddenly asked if I knew of any place in Hamburg where I could live, recover and go to my doctor from there. 'When should I go?' 'Now, as soon as possible!' He got up and retired to his private chambers. I stood near the door with my hands folded. Then he turned to me again and looked at me with infinite love. I had no idea that this was his parting glance for me. I never came so close to him again.

I immediately got on the phone and called the TM-Center in Hamburg. 'Yes, there was a room for free for me.' The Center was a posh villa right on the Outer Alster – a lake in the middle of Hamburg. It was supposed to be used for executive presentations, which unfortunately did not happen. But for me it was a great luck that this house was available (financed by the international Movement). Besides me, five other TMers lived there, with whom I got along well. Several times a week I could hear from my room, how the meditators came to the regular meetings and gathered in the room next to me. I still felt too weak to attend myself.

Maharishi with (from left) Heinz-Peter Specht, Peter Petersen and Hans Vater in the traditional Indian dress

Vedic Monk – Member of the 'Thousand Headed Purusha'

After many months, in April 1982, I asked, via my friend Wolfgang, if I could join the international group again. The answer was, 'Yes, I should come to Boppard.' There, in a rented old monastery building, the Kloster Marienberg, the home of the 'Thousand Headed Purusha', a kind of 'monk-lifestyle' group, had just been started by Maharishi for long-serving and advanced TM teachers. The name 'Thousand-Headed Purusha', later called simply 'Purusha', comes from Rigveda.[28] 'Purusha' means 'person'. The 'thousand-headed' person, who can see and hear in all directions, is an image for the 'Lord of Creation', the Absolute, the ONE Consciousness from which all that is relative arises. The members of the Purusha Group were to devote themselves entirely to their spiritual development, i. e. meditate and practice advanced techniques together.

I have mentioned earlier that, according to Maharishi's teachings and according to concrete experiences, the collective 'program' of many people meditating together creates 'coherence' in the near and far environment. Later, the group was indeed sent to political crisis areas several times to create calming and peaceful vibrations. When I got there, I learned that we would have no contact whatsoever with the female sex, not the slightest contact, not even with the wife of the national leader, an elderly lady.

When they dropped me off in my room and I saw through the window the courtyard and the meter-thick walls of the house, I said to myself, 'Now I am in a monastery!' That was a bit of a shock. Nevertheless, already after a few weeks I felt like a fish in water.

I could not yet participate in the group program. Only healthy people were admitted, because according to Maharishi's teaching, even 'non-infectious' diseases were transmitted to other people, on a subtle level, especially in a situation where everyone was very 'coherent'. I meditated alone in my room, but made sure that I was coordinated time wise with the others. Otherwise, I was fully integrated into the group. I ate with them, studied the Vedic scriptures with them, or whatever Maharishi's assignment was, and did my daily 'walk and talk' with others, the walk through the grounds that belonged to the monastery, a park with old trees on both sides of a small stream. We had a 'buddy-system' and a 'buddy' (a friend) was always with me, especially when I had an errand in town. The park was surrounded by a wall with a WYMS watchman at the only exit.

Otherwise, life in our monastery was by no means ascetic. Most of us had renovated single rooms with carpeting and a newly built shower, so no 'monk cells' were without heating or anything like that! We had a very comfortable routine, slept sufficiently, and the vegetarian food, which everyone helped to prepare in turn, was good and plentiful. The whole atmosphere was very relaxed. There were fixed times for everything: breakfast, long meditation program, eating, walk and talk, studying, and everything proceeded without haste and without pressure.

After I had been living like this for some time, the big moment finally announced: Maharishi wanted to come! For the first time in many, many months I would see him again! I imagined how he would address me separately and inquire about my health. After he arrived, to greet him, I waited halfway up the spacious staircase, which had the character of a castle entrance.

Maharishi had difficulty climbing the stairs. He pulled himself up with his hand on the inner railing, looking down at the steps. He walked past me on the other side of the wide stairs without looking up. I stood there with my flower, with my heart full of anticipation. Then suddenly he turned around, saw me and put his hands together in greeting. I walked over to him and handed him my flower. The bystanders watched intently: How would Maharishi treat me now? The greeting was not quite as dreamed; but still! Happiness and disappointment were balanced within me.

The following week we had happy meetings in the big hall, the former church, whose walls and pointed arches had been painted in bright yellow by the Purushas themselves. I was given a seat of honor in the front row, in front of the rather high stage where Maharishi was enthroned on his white-covered sofa. We were working on some advertising copy or large diagrams. This was apparently the way Maharishi sought to anchor knowledge in us at that time.

Soon he left again, but came to visit us more often during the next months. Sometimes 'boat rides' were organized on the nearby Rhine River, which he loved so much. We went out on a large pleasure boat, in whose restoration room we all had plenty of space. On a full moon night, we even went as far as Bonn. During these trips, Maharishi also ordered that I, together with Wolfgang and other dignitaries, sit directly in front of him. The conversations during the boat trips were very relaxed. Everybody could bring up some trivialities.

Once, at the very beginning, there was hope that the old situation would be restored. From Seelisberg came the message that I should come to Maharishi. I was congratulated. Apparently, it was starting again. On the first day of my stay in Seelisberg, I was standing just below in the entrance area of the Kulm when Maharishi stepped out of the elevator. I put my hands together and bowed deeply. Somehow, at that moment I had the idea that this would be appropriate and appreciated by Maharishi. But when I looked up again, he had already moved on. The next day I was instructed by a secretary to go back to Boppard.

Had Maharishi just wanted to check how I was doing? Was he disappointed with me? I never found out. So, I had no choice but to continue my monastic Purusha life.

At some time there was a city fair on the Boppard square below the monastery walls. That day Maharishi came for a visit again. While he was speaking, we were at the same time enjoying the 'Tschingderassabum' German brass band music coming through the windows. But Maharishi appeared indignant afterwards, about the disturbance. We should have spoken with the city council to request a pause in the music.

After the week of 'Silence' in January 1983, Maharishi invited us to a big Course in Chianciano in Tuscany. The entire Purusha group went there and took the night train to Italy. When Maharishi arrived at his hotel, many followers stood in the entrance hall to greet him with a flower. This time I did not get to stand in the front row. When I saw Maharishi getting out of his car in the distance, I was suddenly overcome by a huge fear. As he approached, my fear became stronger and stronger and, maybe it was because of this fear itself or because I actually did something wrong, in any case, when Maharishi passed me, he looked past me as if by chance and overlooked my flower. So, I ran behind the queue, the only one still with a flower in his hand, but I could not reach him anymore. It was clear that this was no accident. Something had gone terribly wrong. After a few days. Maharishi was in a friendly manner again.

Spring and summer went by. Apart from my deep impatience to get well again, I felt completely at home in the Purusha life. It was tailor-made for me, or so it seemed.

For 'Guru Purnima', the important Vedic full-moon festival in July, Maharishi was with us once again. He himself performed a puja in front of the image of his Master, Guru Dev, during the celebration. Afterwards he sat down on his sofa, which, this time quite unusually, stood right next to the small puja altar. Each of us went forward to put a flower on the altar and bowed to the image as was customary. Since Maharishi was sitting right next to it, some felt urged to bow to Maharishi also while getting up. When it was my turn to bow to Guru Dev, I hesitated for a moment. I was aware that Maharishi usually subordinated himself completely to his Master and did not want separate reverence. Nevertheless, since he had obviously accepted the homage of some this time, I was unsettled.

The moment I turned to him, he calmly pointed with his left hand to the image of Guru Dev and hinted. This is your master. My friend K.-E. told me afterwards that it was quite different with him: When he showed his homage to Maharishi also, he beamed at him!

Many years later, when I was no longer a Purusha member, I was told in a channeling session that Guru Dev had been my Master for many lifetimes and that he had given Maharishi the task to take care of me in this life and move forward. This is truly what he has done.

Greece and Italy

In late summer, Maharishi suddenly announced a journey for all. We were
to go to the Greek island of Kos, which was near the Turkish mainland.
We did not ask why, but later it became clear that it had to do with the
Lebanon crisis. Obviously, our group was supposed to have a harmonizing
influence on the eastern Mediterranean through our group program. On
the way to Kos, we had a few hours' stop in Athens. I walked to the sea
and sat down on the stony shore. Suddenly, to my surprise, I noticed how
I breathed a sigh of relief; somehow a weight fell from my heart. I realized
that I had not really felt free in Boppard after all. I had not expected that.

So, I decided to really enjoy my holiday in Kos. But again, it turned out
differently: I lived in a double room with H., a young and very ambitious
Purusha, who already had a certain leading role. After a few days,
Maharishi himself actually called the telephone in our room, probably
to speak to H. I picked up the phone and after a long time I was finally
speaking to him directly. He also immediately gave me some small orders.
H. did not like that at all, and he tried to squeeze in everywhere, while
I tried to defend my seemingly revitalized position. This created tension
between us.

Finally, Maharishi himself came to Kos. In the days that followed, he
gave me a few more assignments, and I hoped to regain my old position.
Then Maharishi decided to fly to Cyprus, which was even closer to
Lebanon. Many of the veteran top people, former secretaries, and so on,
who had come with him to Kos, flew along. But also a small group of
Purusha members were to come along. I was in that group but 'buddy' H.
was not.

In the Greek section of Cyprus, the whole team lived in a Hilton hotel
together with Maharishi; and he played one of his favorite games with us.
We were supposed to look for hotels all over Cyprus where the Purusha
group could stay permanently to create coherence. I also got on the phone
and actually was assigned one of the best projects of all. Together with
Wolfgang, I went on a day trip to the south, to negotiate with the hotel
owner. Afterwards I was allowed to report to Maharishi, I felt more, and
more hope to be 'in' again. But in the end, the hotel project was cancelled.

Soon our small Purusha team of four was sent to Pescara in southern Italy to continue searching for hotels there. Here we hung around for a few weeks, ate well in our hotel, to which we had given hope that it would be permanently occupied by a large group. From time to time, we reported to Maharishi by phone. Finally, the negotiations stagnated.

Since we were getting more and more bored, I, as the leader of our group, decided in my impatience that we should leave now. The others agreed. Already before that, Rome had been envisioned as the next stop in accordance with Maharishi, and I had already made preliminary arrangements with Bruno Romano for our stay. Now we had only to get the final okay for our move. I called several times to Seelisberg, where meanwhile Maharishi resided again. But he was always unavailable. Finally, we were put off until the next day. I was so sure of myself that I made all the preparations to take the only bus of the day to Rome the next morning.

Early in the morning, however, Ior Guglielmi, the Italian TM Governor who had been assigned to us as a negotiator, came to my room and said he had an idea how we could bring the negotiations to a good conclusion after all. I did not want to know anything about it; I just wanted to leave here, especially since we had already prepared everything for departure. I suppressed the negative feeling.

The time was approaching when the bus was to leave. Still I had not reached Maharishi. I was told on the phone that he was in a meeting and could not be disturbed. I asked someone to go to the meeting room and contact Nandkishore, who would probably be sitting on the stage next to Maharishi, so that he could perhaps ask a quick question in passing.

In the meantime, the bus had arrived. I instructed my group to put all the suitcases inside the bus, get on the bus themselves and wait. I myself waited endless minutes on the phone. Finally, my messenger came back and told me that Nandkishore had said we could go. This was not what I needed, because Nandkishore was only a secretary, albeit the top one, and could only make limited decisions. Nevertheless, I took this as a green light and rushed to the bus. As soon as I jumped on, the door closed and we left.

I felt this as one of my courageous actions in the sense of, 'What's right will get support from Nature.' A somewhat queasy feeling remained nevertheless. Especially since I had not been able to contact Bruno in Rome to announce our arrival, because the situation had been unclear until the last second. He did not even know on which day and at which time we would arrive. I had trusted Nature again. As a back up, I still had dozens of telephone numbers of TM teachers and contact persons in Rome, from my secretarial time.

We enjoyed the bus ride through the Apennines, with its scattered little towns and white villages that stuck like bird's nests at the top of the mountains. I had never known that Italy had such idyllic landscapes. Finally, we arrived in Rome near the central station. We dragged our luggage to the station hall, and I called Bruno. However, he was not there. I called the next person on my address list. He was not there either. And so it went on one by one. Nobody was at home. Being a Saturday afternoon, no Roman stays in his apartment, I was told later.

That was an awkward situation; especially since our meditation time had long since begun and our nervous systems were attuned to this time of deep rest. Therefore, we had to look for places on some hard benches next to smoking travelers to begin our meditation program. More and more I felt that my decision had been wrong and that I had not received any 'nature-support'.

After meditation, I called Maharishi and actually got him on the phone. I told him that we were in Rome. The first question he asked was, 'What about the hotel in Pescara?' Then everything was clear: our departure had been a mistake. Once again, I had thought too superficially. It probably was not about the hotels at all in the end. We should probably just be in southern Italy on the Adriatic Sea for some subtle strategic reasons. I told Maharishi that we were sitting here at the train station and could not reach anyone. Maharishi and Nandkishore, who overheard the conversation, laughed: 'You haven't even managed to organize your own reception! Ha, ha, ha.'

After this conversation, I tried Bruno again. Now someone picked up the phone immediately, and he made sure that the city's TM Center was opened to us, which was located nearby at Piazza di Spagna. The transport there was not without difficulty, but finally we rummaged through the crowd of people who celebrated the weekend in this famous square near the Spanish Steps and settled in the Center.

What were we actually supposed to do in Rome? I did not know and we had nothing to do there. We went sightseeing every day. Nandkishore gave me the order to buy corals for Dr. Dwivedi, which he needed for his Ayurvedic medicine. I threw myself into research and became a coral expert. But when I tried to tell Maharishi about it by phone, he declined. This was Nandkishore's project, and he was not interested.

After a few weeks, we spoke with Maharishi again. The conversation was very relaxed. He suggested that we should go to Como, where our Movement ran an academy. I agreed enthusiastically. We would have done enough sightseeing by now. Maharishi laughed. He even wanted to send his private plane to transport us to Como. Later it turned out that he did not approve the plane when talking to our Seelisberg travel service agent, so we finally had to go by train. In Como, we were just hanging around again and had no assignment.

Then one day I actually got an assignment from Maharishi, albeit in response to my own question. Together with Reinhard B., who meanwhile filled my former secretary position, I was to give the final instructions and secret instructions at a TTC. This was an honor and a very trustworthy task. Reinhard therefore came to Como, where the TTC had been running for months. In the following days, I noticed on several occasions with melancholy that Maharishi was talking mainly to Reinhard and not to me, even though we were on the phone together.

In the meantime, my three teammates traveled back to Boppard. All of the Purusha group had long since left Greece, and they had been trying for weeks to get visas for America, where a large gathering of 7,000 Sidhas was soon to take place. According to Maharishi's teaching, such a large group could create coherence for the whole world.

While I was still teaching the TTC with Reinhard, we actually managed to get these visas. Everybody flew to the USA, including my three colleagues, who were just able to jump on the departing train that was leaving for the airport. When Reinhard and I, it was now November 1983, returned to Boppard, the whole house was empty except for a single TM teacher who acted as caretaker. We looked for the most comfortable rooms and after a short time, I started to enjoy the silence. In the meantime, I had regained enough strength to go on short hikes.

America – a 'Taste of Utopia'

Nevertheless, of course I wanted to be in America. Then one day, Reinhard and I got the okay to come to the USA. We managed to persuade the airline to let us take the whole typesetting system, with many large machines and computers, as luggage for a little extra charge. For this purpose, I got carnets,[*29] (customs documents) filled out in my name, which later forced me to make a huge organizational effort to prove that the equipment had been re-exported out of the country. Nobody had thought of confirming the re-export into the carnets. So, I had to make sure that we, in fact even I personally, did not have to pay the customs duty. But Maharishi had already remarked at the beginning, 'Why do we need carnets at all? They are American devices anyway?' Nevertheless, I had not heeded him; I just thought that I had to go the correct way. But already on the outbound flight, I noticed that nobody asked for the papers. So I finally got a lesson here again.

Directly after our arrival in Washington, D. C., in the large refurbished hotel where Purusha was housed, Reinhard and I were allowed to meet Maharishi in his suite. He turned mainly to Reinhard, and I felt only more or less tolerated, as a quasi-assistant to Reinhard.

After a few weeks in Washington, the whole Purusha group was shipped, via Maharishi's private plane, to Fairfield, Iowa. The private university of our Movement was there, on the grounds of which, the 7,000th assembly was to take place. A gigantic temporary assembly hall made of sheet metal had been built there, where the men would 'fly'. The women 'flew' in the two 'Golden Domes, the golden yellow dome-shaped 'flying' and assembly halls that had been built years ago for the daily 'flying' program of the students and professors. The whole thing was a huge event. However, I could not yet fully participate because I still felt quite weak and sickly. In addition to my liver weakness, I now had a flu, which kept me in my room. From there I watched every morning as countless buses with participants who lived off-campus rolled into the university grounds.

I missed the only major meeting where Maharishi appeared in person. I did not expect him to interrupt his 'silence,' which usually lasted until January 7 or 8. But since many participants had to leave, he actually came out on January 6 and unexpectedly stepped onto the stage of the great hall just as the festive closing ceremony was taking place. The next day a big group photo was arranged; but again, I didn't go because I didn't think I would be able to stand being out in the cold for very long, health wise.

By the way, during the climax of the gathering, when Maharishi was still 'in silence,' there was an extreme cold of -33° Celsius, plus a storm, which, with the so-called 'wind-chill factor,' resulted in a combined chill effect of about -66° C for the body. I never had experienced such a thing before nor did I ever experience it again afterwards. One day even Bevan Morris, the leader of the whole project, decided to stop the flying together and traveling with the buses because it would be too dangerous. Some of the participants actually froze their noses, even though they were all completely bundled up. Maharishi was displeased with Bevan's decision afterwards, because the coherence of the joint flying program should have been maintained at all costs in favor of the global coherence-effect.

Despite this small interruption, the effect was obviously there. Scientific analysis of newspaper reports actually showed an enormous increase in peaceful and healthy tendencies all over the world, during this period. The extreme cold in the USA was obviously a side effect of the coherence created, similar to what happened at the Baltic Sea, Weissenhäuser Beach, at that time.

After the 7,000 Assembly, Maharishi sent all the Purushas out into the world in teams of four. He called this the 'Global March' to make governments and the public aware of the possibility of creating true peace through his Consciousness Technology. I had signed up for Thailand. But just before I left, Maharishi decided that I should not expose myself to such health risks again. So, I stayed behind and had plenty of time to hang out. In a way, I enjoyed the familiar atmosphere of a university, browsed the library and was only moderately bored.

Maharishi himself also stayed in Fairfield for quite some time. He lived in one of the larger houses on the university campus and had his building surrounded by a high wooden fence including a watchtower, on which a hired guard was constantly posted. It soon became clear that such measures were not unjustified. Similar to the spiritual community of Osho, our Movement had long been under the scrutiny of the American secret service. Osho was put in jail in the USA a few years later, under some pretext, for alleged immigration offences, and, according to his own statement, there they put the insidious poison thallium into his food, so that after years he could no longer stand the strong pain caused by this and decided to leave the body.

I suspect that something similar was intended regarding Maharishi. When he, much later, heard about Osho's death and his story, he supposedly said, 'They wanted to do this with me, but they could not get me.' In Fairfield, bailiffs came to the gate of his residence in order to ask him to come along and appear before the court. Nandkishore spoke to the people and told them that Maharishi was just in a meeting and he could not interrupt it. Please come back tomorrow. The next day, however, Maharishi was no longer there and disappeared without a trace. Later I asked my friend F., who had been there, to tell me the details. That evening Maharishi called Nandkishore and F. and told F. to prepare a car for a drive. Absolutely nobody should know anything, except the cook who was also coming along. In order not to attract attention, nobody should take even the smallest luggage with him. Nevertheless F. quickly grabbed a clean spare shirt and put it in his briefcase. A few days later Nature rebuked his disobedience by tearing up the shirt in the washing machine. F. drove the car with the three passengers out of the property and Maharishi was not seen for three quarters of a year. Strangely enough, the four were still living somewhere in the USA, in a house or Hotel together, a heavenly time for my friend F., as he could be very close to Maharishi and eat together at the table with him, something the rest of us could only dream about. Even at the end of the year, when we were all in the

Philippines, practically no one knew where Maharishi was. I learned later that at that time he was staying on the top floor of a fine hotel in Manila, very close to our group, where he met at least some of the top people of the Movement. But at that time, I was no longer one of them.

Boppard – director of a meditation academy

This disappearance of Maharishi took place at a time when I was no longer in the USA. One day he had called me together with Wolfgang E., Heinz-Peter S. and Hein Geelfink, who had also stayed in Fairfield, to the intercom and told us to go back to the monastery in Boppard and to set up a meditation academy for men there. We set off as ordered, although the three others were not particularly enthusiastic about this idea. So they were happy that a few days after our arrival in Germany we got permission from 'International' (i. e. Maharishi) to go to the big European meditation course in Yugoslavia. With Hein's Mercedes, we strolled south, stopped in Venice and then enjoyed the relaxed Course atmosphere on the Adriatic Sea, without getting particularly involved, because we were only 'Guests of honor.'

After returning to Boppard, I was impatient to begin the academy project. But Wolfgang and Heinz-Peter did not feel like it. They soon left, and I was left alone with Hein, who was in his comfortable room with a bath. He needed something like that. He mostly sat in front of the TV and enjoyed the peace and quiet. Hein was responsible for the finances. He understood a lot about that. So, I visited him regularly in his hermitage, showed him the bills, which he then looked at with his head tilted at an angle and wobbling a little back and forth. Then he usually said in his characteristic Frisian tone, 'Jo, seems we'll have to pay that.'

For all other aspects of the project, I had a completely free hand. I designed information material, recruited course instructors, inspired the TM Center and organized a big opening ceremony with all the dignitaries of the German Movement, of course with a steamboat trip on the Rhine. Little by little, the first Purusha teams returned from their 'Global March' and I engaged them to help with the service for our course guests. Fortunately, they were happy to do so, and gradually we gained a good reputation, so that soon, at least on the weekends, we had quite a few participants.

This summer of 1984 turned out to be one of the happiest periods of my life. I had an assignment again, and a limited and well-defined one at that. I was the boss again, that suited me. I could use my skills and succeeded. One day, however, this pleasant time also came to a sudden end. Maharishi called, from which corner of the world no one knew, and said that we should close Boppard and all the Purushas should fly to the Philippines. Therefore, I called everyone together and we organized a quick and quiet closure.

Philippines

In the Philippines, all the Purushas met again, as well as thousands of meditating 'Sidhas' from all over the world. You may recall that President Marcos was the controversial leader of the Philippines at that time. He ruled with cruel and unjust oppression, so it was said. To everyone's surprise, Maharishi had now sided with him and apparently wanted to save his regime by creating coherence. We meditators were not accustomed to questioning Maharishi's instructions; we trusted him unquestioningly. He would make the right decisions. The fact was that Marcos had indeed asked Maharishi for help, and Maharishi apparently saw an opportunity here to demonstrate the effectiveness of his Consciousness Technology, that is, a large coherence-creating group.

When we were there and could see the situation up close, it soon appeared to us that the world press had deliberately and with evil intent totally distorted the situation. While Marcos may not have been an orphan in his methods, I cannot judge that, I'm sure that he was an intellectually very high standing personality, who had rendered great service to his country and, I believe, still wanted the best for his state.

Although he came from one of the rich families of landowners – the leaders before him and after him did so too! – he had begun to initiate land reforms, in contrast to his opponent who followed him in power. I suspect that he was shot in the foot precisely because he wanted to soften the contrast between rich and poor through his policies, thereby depriving communist revolutionary aims of their ground. So, they quickly tried to render him harmless and to set a revolution in motion by inciting the population, especially the students. It was not that difficult; I remember it from 1968. It was perhaps a little more difficult for the more relaxed Filipinos than for us Germans. We could see that the relatively small anti-Marcos demonstrations were more of a happening for the young people, where they blew up firecrackers and had a lot of fun. In the press, one then read about huge demonstrations and attacks.

It looked as though Maharishi did not succeed with his aims. Marcos had to go after all. The opposition in his own ranks, especially in the military, was already too strong. My personal theory, however, is that Maharishi achieved about exactly what he had set out to do. There was no communist revolution, as the other side would have liked and planned. The transfer of power was peaceful. Basically, everything stayed the same, except another rich family came to power. The day after Marcos' resignation, the world press turned to another 'grievance'; I think it was about South Korea.

Our time in the Philippines was not without danger. One of the hotels where TM meditators stayed was even set on fire. Interestingly, Maharishi had previously instructed that just this hotel should be evacuated, but the women who were leading that group refused to move out because it was such a beautiful and comfortable place. The hotel where the Purusha was staying was also surrounded by picketers and we could only enter and leave through the back exit. Maharishi finally ordered that we were only allowed to go out on the street in large groups.

This caused some difficulties for many of us, because in the meantime we had discovered the Filipino miracle healers. I still remember how S. and I secretly took a taxi soon after our arrival and drove out of town to one of the healers. And then, who should come in when we had taken a seat in the waiting room? The other two members of our four-member Purusha board, that is, the governing body to which I belonged at that time. We had not even taken them into our confidence. For we had to fear that with this action we would be considered 'off the program', that is, not allowed. We risked at least the loss of our high position as leaders of the

Purusha group. But later it turned out that Maharishi was very relaxed about 'visits to the healers. When one of our doctors approached him, he said, 'Let them get a taste of the local healing tradition.'

At the monastery in Vlodrop, Holland

After the stay in the Philippines, Purusha reunited in Vlodrop in Holland. Our new domicile was a massive and extensive Franciscan monastery built at the beginning of the century, which the Dutch national leader had in the meantime purchased for us. When our group arrived there, I looked up at the Gothic pointed arches in the entrance hall and thought, 'Oh, I think I can live quite well here.' And in fact, I stayed there, with an interruption of 6 months, for almost seven years. But the day after our arrival, we first went on a 14-day trip to The Hague, where a large coherence meeting with 6,000 TM-Sidhas had been organized. Of course, I had not been informed anything about that either, I was a 'nobody' now. In 'The Hague', I enjoyed the privilege of staying at Maharishi's hotel.

In The Hague, Maharishi appeared in public again for the first time after his disappearance in the United States. At a festive meeting in the large airport hall, he announced a new world government, where 'ministers' and 'sub-ministers' –mostly 'Purushas' were installed. I was not among them. I guess I did not want to do it anyway. I thought, 'Let them do it.' And it soon became clear that the new ministers did not have much to say and do, only the 'chief ministers' were given a certain representative function and authority.

Ironically, Reinhard, now the head of everything, soon gave me a job in the communications department, where I had to correct and sometimes reject all outgoing letters, including those from the ministers. In some cases, this caused resentment, because the ministers felt their dignity had been offended. I had a particularly hard time with E.S. when I refused to let a bombastic circular letter that he wanted to send to governments go through.

Those days in The Hague were very happy for me, although it was freezing cold. At one point, I was desperate to get to the sea and walked along the empty streets in a thick clothing, looked through the low windows into the living rooms, which were still decorated for Christmas, and finally reached the beach, where I listened to the calming sound of the sea. After long months in the tropics, I felt at home again.

From The Hague, I went back to Vlodrop, where I had a rather quiet time until 1991, only interrupted once by a six-month trip to India. Still I hoped to work for Maharishi again one day. However, in the beginning at least, I was still too weak. I could not lift anything heavy, and I could not even stand for a long time! Fortunately, my job in the communications department was quite easy to manage.

I took walks in the surrounding forest and studied popular management literature. The latter was a hobby of mine; ridiculously enough, I hoped that I might be able to use this knowledge again in a management position in the movement. Except for a short period of one and a half years, 1999 and 2000, this never happened. But the effect of these studies was fruitful. By being mentally involved in the field of management, I apparently lived out these Sanskaras[*30] on the spiritual level without having to become active on the outer level. In any case, after about two years I had left behind the need to manage something. This experience showed me: You do not always have to fulfill wishes in the outer plane. Often a purely mental experience of the corresponding area is sufficient.

India

In the summer of 1986, I came into contact with a self-healing method that was very effective for me. Through it my liver weakness disappeared within a few weeks. This in turn enabled me to participate in the journey of Purusha to India.

India! Five years ago, I would have loved to stay there forever, but now the memory of the illness was still in my bones and I could not enjoy it fully. Nevertheless, this stay was a very important experience for me. For six months, we Purusha lived together with several thousand participants, 'Sidhas', from all over the world, in a huge ashram outside Delhi. There Maharishi, in the desert-like development area called Noida, which we already knew since the Dipavali celebration in 1980, had meanwhile raised into a small town. The most striking buildings there were two large 'pentagons', one of which was still more or less a shell, and Maharishi's large house, the 'Kutja', where he held his private meetings and smaller gatherings. In addition, there were large living areas of simple one-story houses for a few thousand young Pandit disciples who received training in reading, writing and Vedic recitation in this ashram.

I was accommodated in a Pentagon room together with Hein, but when the rainy season was over, I preferred to sleep in a tent outside at night. These tents were so intelligently constructed that the cool night air could always pass freely. Anyway, the nights under the open sky in India are among the most delightful things I have experienced in my life. In the distance you could hear mostly dogs barking and some kind of celebration with music, singing and drums; but all this was based on a deep silence and peace, which I have hardly ever experienced in the West.

Almost every evening, when the sun had already set, Maharishi's 'lecture' took place outside in the garden in front of his 'Kutja'. Sometimes the Shankaracharya was also present. He was given a place of honor, practically a throne, while Maharishi more or less sat at his feet. These meetings often lasted until late into the night. As a former secretary, I could usually sit in a seat of honor in the front rows. The lectures, of course, dealt with Vedic knowledge, which Maharishi wanted to revive especially in its country of origin, India. Sometimes the Shankaracharya also spoke, and Maharishi translated, as it seemed to me, quite freely, large passages summarizing in a few words.

During the day, we Purusha sat together under trees in working groups and studied the Vedic scriptures. Each group concentrated on one of the approximately 40 fields of knowledge of Vedic literature. I had chosen 'Dhanurveda', the knowledge of the art of war, because it was the closest, according to my feeling, to management theory. I was a little sorry that I missed 'Jyotish', Vedic astrology; but the corresponding group was completely overcrowded anyway. However, in the last few weeks of the course I attended a Jyotish beginner's course with an advanced American student, bought Jyotish books and started to get into it.

The most beautiful thing during these six months was the rehearsal of the 'Veda Lila', a kind of play (Sanskrit 'lila') that was supposed to show the origin of the Vedas and their branches from the ONE Ocean of Consciousness. Maharishi had laid out the content in broad outlines, but a group of gifted Purushas had fleshed out the text and, above all, underlined it with beautiful melodies.

Again, and again the piece was rehearsed, with Purushas dressed in elaborate and shiny costumes, who performed Vedas on stage, and often Maharishi would come to serve as the director of the play. The chants were so catchy that many, including myself, sang them almost all day. Even months later, when I was back in Vlodrop, I was always in a state of bliss when these songs went through my mind. The climax of all this rehearsal was a full moon night, when Maharishi again watched the spectacle and made comments. He sat opposite the main stage on a small platform that had been built for him, surrounded by his close associates, with whom he had discussions in between.

The location was a bit confusing and I managed, skillful as I still was in these things, to work my way up to this platform from behind, so that I finally came to sit right next to his sofa and could bathe in his aura. There I was of course totally happy, especially as he looked at me in a friendly manner, at times. The next night the play was to be repeated, but Maharishi didn't come anymore.

Finally, the end of the course was approaching, it was now around Christmas 1986. Not all of Purusha had to return, you could apply to stay. But I was one of the departing students. My heart ached that my old dream of living in India for a long time was not fulfilled, especially since the great Kumbha Mela was due in Allahabad in the spring. Many years before, I had often dreamt of this greatest spiritual festival in the world, where every twelve years, many of the saints and enlightened beings of India are gathered where the Ganges and Yamuna rivers meet, and where many millions of Hindu believers take their holy bath in the Ganges on a special day. But I had decided to go back to Europe in spite of everything. Life under these poor hygienic conditions was too exhausting for me.

The evening before our group left, Maharishi met the departing participants in his Kutja as usual. Every single one went to him in the front. When I got there and presented him with a beautiful rose, I naturally expected a sign of recognition and a few special words, such as: 'Are you healthy again?' Therefore, a beaming 'Yes!' immediately came out of me when he had hardly finished the first sentence. But all he had said was, 'Are you going back, too?' I realized that my beaming of joy hadn't been so appropriate.

Usually at the end of the personal conversation, Maharishi would return a flower from the bundle of flowers given to him by devotees. This time, however, he had none in front of him, and so, as a farewell gift, he gave me back my own flower in an almost ceremonial ceremony after only a few words.

Much later, almost fifteen years later, it occurred to me that this gesture had been something like an official farewell, after the unofficial, loving smile in 1981 in his suite in Seelisberg.

Vlodrop again, 1987 to 1991

After India, I spent four and a half quiet and orderly years in our monastery in Vlodrop. During this time, I felt quite comfortable and at home. By now, things were not as strictly regulated as it was in Boppard at the beginning. You could go shopping in Heinsberg or in Mönchengladbach. As long as it did not happen too often, as long as you had a 'buddy' with you and as long as you were back for the 'program', nobody said anything.

Nobody said anything to me anyway, because I still held a position of honor. Besides, I was mostly among the eager ones and followed the 'rules' as precisely as possible. This corresponded to my nature and also to my ambition. After all, I wanted to be enlightened as soon as possible. And how do you best achieve this? By meticulously following the master's instructions, so I thought.

I felt fully integrated into the group and never doubted for a minute that I would spend most my life in the lap of the TM Movement and especially Purusha. My two most important occupations during these four years were exposure to Jyotish and later Sanskrit. As I said, I had already started studying Jyotish in the last weeks of my stay in India. To my astonishment, this knowledge flowed into me like warm milk with honey. Everything I read I immediately kept in my memory.

1990 was a not such a good year for me. Nothing really bad happened, except that I twisted my foot so badly that my ankle broke and I had to walk around with crutches for half a year. But much worse was that I constantly felt unhappy, miserable and insecure. Maharishi had just returned to Vlodrop for some time after a longer stay in India, and to my concern he even invited couples and women to our 'monastery' who were also allowed to live here. The whole Purusha-feeling there gradually went down the drain.

Guests from outside were constantly coming, often friends from the past. I could have been happy; but I felt so miserable and strange in this world that I could hardly look them in the eye. A small consolation was to know from my Jyotish constellation chart that I was just in the worst planetary phase of my life. So, I could at least hope that my inner situation would change for the better after one year.

Sent away from Vlodrop!

And so, it happened in a certain way. The next summer I was shocked by the fact that Maharishi sent the German members of Purusha away from Vlodrop. We were to ensure coherence in the new Eastern European states. Since Maharishi had already sent the Americans and then the British away years ago and did not even want to have them as guests in his ashram in Vlodrop, I knew that for us, the large international Purusha group was no longer to be together, and with that went our proximity to Maharishi. We would now only be national fringe groups. I still remember how, after our long farewell meeting, I hung on with my friend Wolli and said, 'This is the end.' He could not say anything about it because he knew it was true. One sad morning we German Purushas went to Düsseldorf by bus to fly to Berlin from there. As we drove through the ugly outskirts of Düsseldorf, I felt on the one hand, that I had to protect myself from this strange world. I was so used to the safe monastic life far away from the stress of the cities.

On the other hand, I remember that a very quiet breath of joy arose. The relative life seemed to have its charms somehow. The large group of like-minded people in Vlodrop had given me a good foothold, but on the other hand had been quite fixed in their whole thinking and feeling. Everything had revolved around Maharishi. I spoke and thought essentially only what was 'allowed', believing that these were my own thoughts.

The forthcoming stay far away from the monastic headquarters suggested the possibility of new freedom and vitality. Nevertheless, I was by no means happy. And for me, the six to eight months at our new place remained quite joyless. This was due to the whole GDR-feeling in the former holiday resort Wendisch-Rietz at Scharmützelsee, where we lived in small summer cottages and a concrete block building, which had served as a children's recreation home before. The scenically beautiful area was and remained steeped in the desolation of the old regime. I hope that we nevertheless achieved something for the softening of the atmosphere in the old GDR. That was our task – Maharishi had told us.

We had been given a special assignment. We were to establish Ayurveda centers in all major German cities. Maharishi had gone through all the details with us in detail at our big farewell meeting, at which we only connected with him via video conference. Large impressive houses were to be found everywhere where Ayurveda treatments, TM introductions and a whole spectrum of Movement activities would be given. Maharishi, somewhat reluctantly, had even participated in the calculation of income and expenditure. It seemed to be a very important project that we should work on in our 'spare time' (outside our long program hours).

I already suspected a little bit, that it might be just an occupational therapy again. A small hint that it could be so happened due to a mishap of the video crew. When the meeting was over, they switched off the connection too late, so that we got an unofficial remark of Maharishi, which was actually only meant for the people around him. He said something like, 'A very elaborate farewell party.'

Moreover, during the meeting it became clear that the Ayurveda centers could hardly be profitable for the labor-intensive treatments, as we could not impose arbitrarily high prices on the public. Until then only one or two of our Ayurveda clinics all over Germany could do more than just survive, and this with a large proportion of voluntary work. How then could tens of clinics survive at the same time, which would have had to share the limited potential of clients? But you never knew. Maybe Maharishi was really serious this time. We had no right to question his instructions.

And so, we threw ourselves into the work. Maharishi's demands on the standard of the houses were very high. Nevertheless, we managed to find a number of beautiful houses in Germany which were even available. When Maharishi was informed about this, he promptly set the criteria higher, so that almost all our 'A' grade houses had to be downgraded to 'B'. But we were not discouraged and intensified the search. Even so, Maharishi was apparently not satisfied. He never spoke directly with us, only indirectly sending us messages that did not exactly indicate his approval.

And then one day, Lüder, who, before, had worked in the purchasing department, stood up during a meeting and said that in similar situations, Maharishi was already satisfied if people had found only one supplier who had what they were looking for. Lüder suggested that we should simply collect newspaper clippings with corresponding real estate offers from all over Germany and send them to Maharishi, regardless of whether the conditions were acceptable, independent of any pre-negotiations.

I thought, 'You can't fool Maharishi like this and give him Potemkin villages!' Nevertheless, most followed this suggestion. Very quickly, we had a considerable amount of newspaper clippings together. One afternoon we faxed a summary to Maharishi's secretariat. To make sure that the papers were well received, we called the secretaries. The secretary who was on the line said, 'Just a moment!' Silence, then Maharishi himself came on the phone! That was the first time!

Our team members told him about the 108 offers they had just faxed through. Maharishi was extremely pleased. He said, 'This is what I expect from the Purusha: Fast action!' He then asked if the properties were all A-categories. Someone said, 'No, just C, because they haven't been confirmed.' 'Okay, then make it quick.' It was crazy: When we had done solid work, Maharishi had been dissatisfied with us; now, with this farce, he was totally happy. Now it should have been clear to every one of us that Maharishi did not expect any concrete results, only that we were busy, with his wishes in mind. Any concrete success, however, he choked off and prevented.

It is interesting that in the following years Ayurveda clinics sprang up like mushrooms everywhere in Germany, only 'unfortunately not from our Movement. Many of us were annoyed that other organizations had copied Maharishi's ideas and were making money off them. I, on the other hand, suspect that Maharishi intended exactly that. He wanted to revive Ayurveda throughout the world. Our Purusha group with its mind power was a means to an end for him. What we had done in Wendisch-Rietz was something like a yagya, a kind of ritual to create a targeted effect in the collective consciousness. Maharishi had never considered it his or our task to be successful on the outer level or even to earn money.

1992 to 1996

We cruised through the winter of 1991/92 quite well. At times, we could walk on the ice of the Scharmützelsee. We fed the gulls and the hooded crows. The common meal in our 'restaurant' was nice. In April, it was suddenly announced, 'We should go to England.' There the 'Natural Law Party', the newly founded political branch of our Movement, was standing for election for the first time.

In a new development area in Skelmersdale near Liverpool, an 'Ideal Village' had existed for years, a community of TM meditators and Sidhas with their own school and so on. A very harmonious and peaceful little village. Apart from us Purushas, meditators and Sidhas from all over Europe had been invited here, and we all did our daily meditation and flying programs together in the 'Dome', a now completely overcrowded domed building in the middle of the village. Of course, we hoped that through our group program we would soften the collective consciousness of England and make it ready from within to vote for our Party.

The Purusha group lived in a dormitory in Southport and we took the bus to Skelmersdale every morning. The whole setup was quite uncomfortable for us and eating from a commercial kitchen with plastic plates and cutlery was not very attractive. But I enjoyed the simple kindness of the people. It was good to get to know this country and to see that the prejudices that were still deeply rooted in Germany were completely unjustified. The English seemed to me to be much more cordial and helpful than the Germans.

The day of the elections was approaching. We were all excited and hoped for at least a few percent of the votes for the Natural Law Party, ideally even for the entry of 'our' candidate into the House of Commons. On election evening, there was a big meeting of everyone in the hall of the 'Dome'. Maharishi was not present, but was connected to us by conference phone. Someone announced that 'our' party had received very few votes; not even all meditators could have voted for them. Maharishi was disappointed, almost depressed, or at least he pretended to be.

The first part of the session was in a depressed mood. Toward the end, however, Maharishi again began to plan the party's participation in elections in other countries and to cheer our optimism. I had believed in the Party. I am quite sure that he did never even think of an external political success of our Party. And if this had happened, he would probably have dissolved the Party immediately with some threadbare arguments. He just wanted to use the political platform to get his message out more effectively.

Israel

From England, we went back to Wendisch-Rietz. We spent another beautiful May at the Scharmützelsee, where even this spiritually exhausted country showed itself from its best side, with many flowers and exploding green. And then came great relief. We were to go to Israel, again to support the election of the Natural Law Party there from the transcendental level.

In Israel, our whole group, all German, was accommodated in the private houses and apartments of the kibbutz-like village of Hararit, a settlement on a mountain in northern Palestine, where the TM meditators of Israel had founded and built up a community years ago. This quartering of an all-German group in a Jewish village was once again a coup d'état by Maharishi, through which probably much karma was worked off.

As we later found out, Maharishi had asked the Israelis in Hararit, 'Do you want to have a Purusha group to support your election campaign?'

The answer was of course an enthusiastic 'Yes'– Purusha had a very good reputation. It was believed to be a strong spiritual influence. And then just before we arrived, Maharishi said an all-German group was coming. There was a lot of lamenting and wailing in many houses. Their worst enemies and persecutors were to come?

But polite as the Israelis were, they could not cancel now. And of course, they could not refuse Maharishi anything. We knew nothing of all this and had no idea how strong the hatred against the Germans and the fear of our people still was in the bones of the Israelis. We were received politely and correctly and were well accommodated.

And we behaved perfectly, except for the fact that some Purushas did not appear regularly for the group program in the relatively narrow and bunker-like 'flying room'. The residents noticed this and, correct and dutiful as they had been brought up themselves, could not understand this at all. We had such an important task, and especially we as Purushas should be an example for all meditators, especially as many of us been taken in and accommodated by victims of the Nazi regime. Oh well. Our boys pulled themselves together a bit more in order to do this. And gradually a deep bond developed almost everywhere through the constant living together.

Three months later, the day before our departure, there was a big celebration on the local tennis court with performances, music and dancing, in which the residents and we participated together. If many had cried before when they heard that the Germans were coming, many cried again now because we had to leave. Much love and intimacy had developed in such a short time. I suspect that through this project some very fundamental issues had been worked out between our two peoples. Perhaps that was the main purpose Maharishi had in mind.

By the way, this stay in Israel was one of the most beautiful times in my life, as it was for many other Purushas. Israel really seemed to be a holy land from its 'scenic' beauty alone. Our village had a beautiful place from which you could sometimes see the Mediterranean Sea in the west. From there a mild and powerful wind always blew over. If one looked to the east, one looked down on the Sea of Galilee as if into a large, dark, infinitely deep eye. In the south one could see as far as Nazareth and in the north as far as Safed, the spiritual center of the Kabbalah.*31 Behind it were the partly snow-covered Golan Heights.

Often, I just sat for hours under one of the still quite tender olive trees and let the sea wind blow around my ears. That was all that really mattered there; I was simply in bliss. In small groups, we also made some excursions, for example, to the Sea of Galilee, to swim in its milky and lovingly flattering water and afterwards dry ourselves in the warm wind, and to visit the holy places we knew from the Bible. Or we went with a somewhat larger group and a guide from our village to the Dead Sea and to Jerusalem, a city that filled me with melancholy and pity, for there was a somewhat sad, or rather mourning, feeling in the people. Each time I returned home moved and deeply touched.

On the full moon of July, 'Guru Purnima', one of the greatest celebrations of our Movement, it was suddenly said, 'Whoever wanted to, was invited to come to Vlodrop.' This was of course a great temptation. But for most people it was simply too expensive or unaffordable, because everyone had to pay for the flight himself. I was torn back and forth. On the one hand, I wished to meet Maharishi and maybe even stay with him for a longer time. On the other hand, I felt so comfortable here and at home. I withdrew into a shell to feel silence and ask deep inside. The decision came quite clearly: 'Stay here!' Nevertheless, it was very painful to hear some friends rolling their suitcases past my window at 5 o' clock the next morning. They would see Maharishi the next day!

America for the second time

The greater part of us stayed, and after a few weeks we went back to America. There, too, the Natural Law Party candidate was running for Presidency in 1992. We arrived in New York early in the morning. In the huge forest areas of the state of New York, our Movement had bought Livingston Manor, a 'Holiday Resort' a long time ago, an extensive complex of hotels and holiday homes with an overgrown golf course and a small lake. The American Purusha had been established there for several years. Some had built small apartments, and someone had built a boat that could be borrowed. There were vast forests in the area. However, they were regrown, the original ones had probably been cut down a long time ago.

In America, everything seemed to be bigger than here. The blueberry bushes, full of beautiful berries, were as tall as a man. One met herds of deer, which were also bigger than ours. They grazed at dusk right in front of my house. I could also watch marmots from the window. In winter there were eerie northern lights shooting up into the sky. It was a world almost like in a picture book. Nevertheless, I was surprised that this abundance of Nature hardly touched me. Why was that? Gradually I realized that America was somehow a superficial country. Everything was outwardly impressive, but something was missing underneath, something that I had experienced so strongly, especially in India, that I had experienced there as Bliss. America, on the other hand, seemed hollow and empty to me.

After six weeks, we went out in small teams to the different cities to support the local candidates spiritually in their election campaign 'on site'. As foreigners, we were not allowed to help practically. But we gave lectures on Transcendental Meditation, in which we used the words 'Natural Law' over and over again to the point of excess, thereby indirectly promoting the party. After a total of three months, we had to leave the country again.

Back in Vlodrop, Maharishi, to my surprise, only gave us two nights to sleep, some of us only one. The first night I slept like a dead man. In the evening Maharishi listened to our reports via intercom. I was able to report in detail on my actions, and Maharishi showed great interest, although nothing had come out of it. Then it was said: 'In the morning, everyone was to fly to Spain.'

I spent the next three months in Almerimar, not far from Almeria, a completely new, friendly holiday resort on the Mediterranean Sea. I lived on the 10th or 12th floor of a huge hotel, directly above the beach and the sea, which at this time of year, now winter 1992/93, was by no means always quiet, but was sometimes whipped up by high waves. In the same hotel once again a big 'coherence meeting' took place with hundreds of meditators and Sidhas from all over Europe. Such gatherings or 'Courses', with long 'rounds', had taken place again and again in the last decades, and always, where some dicey situation had arisen, a war threatened or something similar. But, what should we do here in the peaceful Mediterranean? I still do not know today. We Purushas, at any rate, profited from the situation. We had all the time in the world, went for a walk on the beach every day and looked for colorful pebbles, of which there were plenty here in wonderful colors.

I had the happiest days during the 'Silence' time from January 1 to 7, during which Maharishi, who had stayed at Vlodrop, traditionally went into silence. I strolled silently along the coast with my buddy Rainer and listened to the tingling and crackling sounds of the rising and falling waves, which repeatedly showed me pebbles with new patterns and colors. Twice during these months I also drove with a friend, who had a car, into the interior of the country, with its mountains full of flowering almond trees. And suddenly there was silence! I did not even know after the many weeks by the eternally rushing sea that such a thing existed.

For my birthday, I was given another trip as a present. Four of us went to the mountains, the foothills of Spain's Sierra Nevada. Now I could see the shining sea from high above and also walk alone for half an hour through the almond groves, enjoying the quiet melancholy that filled the air of this deserted part of the country. I came back to our hotel at dusk, completely bliss-soaked and full of quiet happiness.

On the Crimea/Ukraine

Towards the end of our stay, we were told that the whole Purusha would go to Crimea, a peninsula in the Black Sea belonging to Ukraine. There was a lot to do there after the fall of the Berlin Wall to soften the atmosphere. On the Crimea, probably the most popular holiday area of the former Eastern Bloc, we had a good time in the seaside resort Sudak, where we were able to relax and enjoy the sun. We were able to walk around the beach and for the first time in many years saw pretty girls in bikinis. I felt a feeling of liberation, similar to what I had experienced in Athens at that time, and the slight excitement that life might have more in store for us than just living among men and meditating in the room during the day.

I realized that despite, or perhaps because of, the long period of celibacy, women were a huge attraction for me.

After a few weeks, we moved to the capital of the island: Simferopol. There we stayed in a hotel complex, where right next door a teacher training course for meditators from the Eastern Bloc took place, divided into two groups, one for boys and one for girls. The girls were carefully looked after by an Indian teacher and were also busy most of the day. Nevertheless, it was unavoidable that numerous contacts were made between us Purushas and the exceptionally beautiful Russian girls. I also made friends with a seventeen-year-old from Kazakhstan. Her name was Julia. And even years later, I was accused with a wink of the eye that I had been seen walking hand in hand with her along the river. Such a thing was, of course, typically unlikely for a Purusha monk, but by then the Purusha lifestyle had become so relaxed that no admonitions were to be expected.

Despite these nice little changes, life in that very poor country with its still depressed mood was not very pleasant. Our food was insufficient. There was almost always only the standard bread, potatoes, cabbage and butter mixed with margarine. After some time, I felt how this monotonous food weakened me. My buddy and I got used to taking the bus to the market every day. The bus ride cost us only about a penny, due to the highly favorable exchange rate and government subsidies for transportation. At the market, we always found fruit, honey and other specialties, mostly offered by housewives who made money from the fruits of their garden. But for this, they had to pay substantial 'protection money' to the omnipresent mafia. Nevertheless, for us everything was very favorable. Here we 'penniless' monks lived as though we were rich. Corruption was omnipresent, as well as thefts and burglaries.

One day we suddenly got the chance to get away from this oppressive atmosphere. Maharishi was looking for people to go to India to offer and teach the Corporate Development Program (CDP) in companies. We were to be trained for this in Vlodrop first. I applied. One night the Hungarian Attila and I got the okay. We left immediately.

There was only enough time to write a letter to Julia. In Vlodrop we studied the whole structure of the CDP program for several months. I was not really eager to go to India, but I got a visa anyway. Actually, I did not fly, because one day shortly before Christmas 1993 Maharishi told me and three other Purushas that we would go to Hannover before New Year's Day and there we would support the campaign of the Natural Law Party.

We busily whirled around in Hanover for half a year, collected registration signatures for the party, contacted the press and so on. Soon afterwards, Reinhard B., the 'candidate for chancellor' of the German Natural Law Party, offered me to do his press work with him in Vlodrop. So Vlodrop became my residence and place of work again for the next six months, with Reinhard as my boss, who had previously been my subordinate in Seelisberg and who had actually not treated me very understandingly when I had to give up my secretarial job to him because of my illness.

Reinhard was a man of high intellectual and spiritual level. He did his job as party chairman and 'candidate for chancellor' excellently. But as a boss, he was a disaster. That was because he did not trust anyone to accomplish anything on their own. He corrected and checked everything and was accordingly overloaded. By the way, the reaction of the press and television to our Party was surprisingly positive or at least neutral.

USA again

After the election, the results being of course dismal again for our Party, the next Purusha project was immediately on the agenda. Once again, we were to go to America. This time it was not about the Natural Law Party, but about new courses in the American centers and about company presentations. We flew in teams of two, distributed to different cities in the USA.

I ended up in Atlanta, where my buddy Rainer and I had little to do. One day the order came from 'International' that our teams of two should disband and every German Purusha should form a group of four together with three Americans each.

For me, a team in Palo Alto in California's Silicon Valley, where the three Americans were already located, was the obvious choice. I travelled there via Denver, Colorado. It was the first time in many years that I was on the road without a buddy and in a foreign country at that. I was taken to the airport and then left alone. That was really exciting for me at that time, as I had always been 'protected' via the buddy system until then. At the same time, I enjoyed this almost overwhelming feeling of freedom while strolling through the airport shops.

The three Americans I was to work with were all very nice and pleasant people. Purusha-members generally understood each other very well anyway, as we had a common ground of thought through Maharishi's teaching. In Palo Alto, we lived in a small family house all to ourselves.

Silicon Valley was a wealthy upscale area. There was little poverty and little crime, unlike the area in Atlanta from which I had just come. We went about our projects calmly. Essentially, it was about getting TM into companies. It was during these activities that I first noticed that I was experiencing a slight turnaround. In the past, I had always been the forerunner in all projects, driving others and trying to carry them along, but now I began to hold back more and more. I took part in everything, but left the initiative to the others. I relaxed and gave up trying to be first everywhere. Today I have the feeling that this development was more than just letting go. I had moved away from an inner dependence on the Movement.

Before, Maharishi and his teachings had been my only purpose in life and my only support. Without Maharishi's recognition and without the work for him I was nothing. Now, from the depths, the feeling arose. I no longer need the Movement and its recognition. My life and my evolution will go on like this; I am free. At that time, of course, I wasn't so clear about it. Soon my visa expired and I had to leave the USA again.

At Maharishi's summerhouse in Vlodrop

I spent the hot summer of 1995 in Vlodrop. There I had chosen a 'Trotaka job'. Trotaka was the most famous disciple of the Vedic Master Shankara[*32] in the 9th century A.D. He distinguished himself by the fact that he could not follow the lectures and discussions of his Master because of his intellectual limitations, but took care of his Master's physical well-being with utmost devotion, cooked for him, washed his laundry and so on. His devotion brought him after long years of selfless service finally to enlightenment. One day he composed, spontaneously and without pre-schooling, some very deep and metrically perfect Sanskrit verses, which are still preserved today. Trotaka, of which Maharishi often spoke and with whom he compared himself in his relationship with his Master, Guru Dev, was the secret ideal of many TMers, as also mine.

And now the opportunity arose for me to take care of Maharishi's garden house and keep it in good condition. In this small winter garden-like building next to our monastery, Maharishi met on warm summer evenings with selected small groups. This cottage was beautifully furnished, with lovely upholstered bamboo chairs and small tables on exquisite carpets. The beams between the large windows were decorated with flowering ornamental plants. Flower arrangements were placed on the floor and on the tables. These were delivered twice a week to the back gate of the monastery building. I had to pick them up there with an electric cart and drive them to the garden shed, which was in a restricted area.

I was almost always alone when I worked in the house, collecting fallen flowers, rearranging the flower arrangements, sorting out wilted flowers, vacuuming and cleaning. In the heat of this glass-roofed greenhouse, sweating devotedly, I knelt down in the daily Sisyphus work, with Trotaka as my role model. After about three hours of work, the little house shone in perfect order and cleanliness.

Unfortunately, Maharishi never came back there after the first week. But I swallowed that, too, because I had learned that one should not hang on to the fruits of one's labor. Probably Maharishi wanted to give me a special chance of development, or so I thought. When I quit my job at the end of December because I had to go to India, Maharishi used the house regularly again, as I learned later.

As I mentioned earlier, Maharishi went into silence every year from January 1 to 7, locked himself in, fasted, and kept silent. In some years, he would leave his private rooms at midnight between January 7 and 8 and go to his meeting room to receive devotees. The chance to see him at that particularly delicate and holy moment was an insider's tip among the residents of the house; and by no means was it well known, especially since Maharishi did not appear every year. This time my buddy, with whom I was to go to India two days later, reminded me of this opportunity. We inquired. Yes, indeed, a larger room had been set up for waiting. We sat down in it with a few dozen others, each with a flower in his hand. At midnight, people whispered to each other, 'Maharishi has come out to receive people.'

We watched as, first, the dignitaries and top people were called out and allowed to go to the meeting room, which was inside Maharishi's suite. Finally, it was said that everyone could come now and wait outside the suite. It was an exciting moment. In a long queue, we stood in silence enjoying the proximity of the holy rooms in the corridor. Little by little, we moved towards the actual suite.

Finally, I too stood in the doorway to the meeting room, where the special guests meditated in their armchairs. Maharishi was seated on his sofa and I could see his tenderness and frailty; and his eyes, which today radiated a very special love and silent power. I knew from earlier years that, after a week of complete silence, he did not have full control over his voice at that moment and could only speak very softly. Everything was so tender about him, and yet at the same time sacred and invincible. Then it was my turn to go forward to him.

I knelt down before him and handed him my flower. In this situation, I had the vague idea, 'I wonder if he still remembers me? I wonder if he'll give me a sign of recognition.' In this expectation I hesitated perhaps a second, kneeling in front of him and looking at him. He, however, turned his gaze away from me in a completely neutral way towards the door where the next person waiting was standing. It seemed to me like, 'Now, buzz off and let the next one in.' Looking back, it seems to me that his gaze also contained the message: 'What are you still doing here anyway? Are you still hanging around?' You can imagine the stabbing feeling in my heart. I went out and thought, 'Good thing the others didn't see me get taken out by Maharishi.' But at the same time, and this was foolish, I was in a deep bliss. Obviously, it was simply from being in the proximity of Maharishi. Even when he no longer paid much attention to me, he had blessed me after all.

That my time with Maharishi and on Purusha was actually long gone did not occur to me at that time. Maharishi had always stressed the value of Purusha life to us. Therefore, there was no meaningful alternative for me to be outside the Purusha program.

India again

Two days later, I was sitting with Reinhard in the plane to Bombay (Mumbai). There were several other Purusha teams on the same flight. The Minister of Education of Madhya Pradesh, who had been introduced to TM shortly before, had invited us to make presentations in all cities of the state and to encourage the foundation of 'Vedic Universities'. Our coordinators had assigned my buddy Reinhard R. and me to Jabalpur, the largest city of the state, though not its seat of government. We appreciated the honor, especially since Jabalpur was Maharishi's birthplace, as word had quietly got around.

On the plane, I took out one of Maharishi's little books to prepare for the presentations. It was a text that I had studied intensively and enthusiastically while still in Palo Alto. But now, I realized after half a page 'I can't read it anymore. Yes, I actually can't hear it anymore. Always the same thoughts, the same formulations, which we have been using for so many years to excess.'

I said to Reinhard, 'Hey, it seems to me, you have to do the presentations essentially on your own. I can't do it anymore. I can't prepare for it, and I can't present this anymore.' He seemed to understand that and said, 'No problem, I'll take care of it.' But he was certainly a bit shocked, because I had been his great role model and even his instructor for becoming a TM teacher at that time.

India was a wonderful experience again. The car journey through the dry and exotic country; living with a traditional Indian family; then our work with presentations, waiting in desolate offices where dusty furniture and files took your breath away; in between again pushing through the crowds in the market streets with their countless stalls and tents; strange smells, noise, dust and heat. But also, morning bathing in the divine river Narmada with its soft and milky, but pure water, greeting the rising sun and letting it dry you out; excursions into the barren but always delightful landscape.

These three months were a marvelous gift. Some of the happiest hours of my life were the nightly return trip to Bombay in a first-class carriage with an open window. The warm wind blew all night long and massaged my body while I meditated in the yoga seat. The dusty train stations, where passengers slept side by side on the platform and a lazy loudspeaker voice made its announcements. And again, and again endless stretches of deserted land: a deep silence despite the wind rushing in your ears.

Back in Europe

Back in Vlodrop, I got a job in our architecture department after three months. The architecture, in our case that meant, 'Vedic architecture', in Sanskrit called 'Sthapatya-Veda' or 'Vastu', that had become very important to Maharishi for some years. According to this teaching, the correct north-south orientation of a house and its grounds, the correct arrangement of rooms, the entrance located on the right side, the free space in the middle, etc., have a fundamental effect on the clarity of thought, the harmonious emotional life and the health of the inhabitants.

In Israel, I had been able to experience for the first time that there was something to this system. There a young couple had built a house according to Sthapatya Veda principles. When I entered this house, I knew nothing about it. Nevertheless, I immediately noticed what a balanced, gentle, orderly and happy atmosphere there was. The inhabitants told me that they had been holding their village meetings there for some time. Since then, these meetings have been totally harmonious, whereas before that there had always been endless and tough discussions about how best to organize community life.

Since Maharishi had discovered this traditional teaching for himself, it became clear that our monastery building was anything but ideal for living, planning, and happiness. It was diagonal to the north-south direction, the entrance was on the wrong side, and the layout was unfavorable. Therefore, Maharishi ordered the construction or rather the erection of a series of smaller prefabricated houses on our property, aligned according to Sthapatya-Veda, in which the most important employees would live. I was involved in the preliminary work for this project.

Soon a large wooden house was built for Maharishi himself, which was completed in 1997. It was situated in a properly marked out plot of land (Vastu) next to the monastery and became the largest wooden house in the whole of Holland. Soon after its completion, when I came back to Vlodrop after a long absence, I could admire it from outside the grounds. With its wonderful architecture, its golden yellow wood and its well-kept garden it lay in the landscape like a jewel. When I stood on the east side of the site, directly opposite the entrance, I could feel the power of its perfect geometry, which came at me like a laser beam.

I had travelled from Wavre at that time. Maharishi had sent us there, a small town near Brussels, in July 1996. Our official task there was to use our 'coherence' to influence the decisions of the European Commission in Brussels for promoting good. The time in Wavre was boring. We stayed in a hotel in a modern industrial area outside the town. At least it was somewhat quiet there, at night, because all surrounding office buildings were then empty.

Maharishi had given us a pleasant time there, a small subgroup of 15 Purushas, to which I also signed up. We were supposed to look for a site in the Belgian Ardennes for a 'European Capital', a kind of spiritual capital for all of Europe, with a meditation academy, 'flying halls', commercial buildings and living quarters for hundreds of Sidhas. Through my experiences with Maharishi's projects, I immediately had doubts whether this project was really meant to be serious. But one could never know. And besides, it couldn't hurt to take this change from our somewhat austere time in Wavre. And indeed, we spent a wonderful 'holiday' time in a small village in the Ardennes. This rather deserted hull mountain range consisted of wide meadows with grazing cows and large areas of forest, which were brutally exploited for timber production. Every morning we went out into the area armed with maps. In the evening, the whole group met again, and each team reported on the sites they had visited. It was great fun. Maharishi had given us the criteria for the land to search. It should be at least 100 hectares in size and slope gently north or east toward a river or lake. These were guidelines from the Sthapatya Veda. Of course, such areas were hard to find. But finally, we had some possibilities in hand, and our group leader Rik reported to Maharishi on the phone. As had been expected, Maharishi was not very satisfied. 'No, 100 hectares would be much too small; there should be at least 1,000! We did not want to build a small village, but a real European capital!'

So, we looked at the maps again and found that there was only one site in the whole of Belgium that could perhaps meet the criteria. It was a huge, protected state forest on the northern edge of the so-called Hautes-Fagnes, a large upland moor. The reason for this was that, because of its exposed position, it was probably the wettest area in the whole of Europe: all the clouds that came from the sea always rained here first. After we went there with the whole crew, we noticed that it was raining constantly, at least that day. Everywhere, the little brooks, flowing to the north, ran through the forest. The atmosphere was extremely inhospitable due to the altitude, cold and humidity. And of course, it was ridiculous anyway to believe that the state would sell us 1,000 hectares of land there, in its largest forest and nature reserve, or even give us a building permit.

So, my suspicion was once again confirmed that Maharishi was only trying to achieve a 'Yagya' effect, perhaps just playing with us and keeping us busy. In any case, he probably also wanted us to have fun and not take everything too seriously. This became especially clear on one of the last days of our stay. That day, Rik suddenly shot into my room: 'Hans, we have to go to Liège to the airport immediately. Maharishi is sending a helicopter there, and we are supposed to see the grounds we've been exploring, inspecting them from above.'

A few hours later, Rik and I, together with the top architect of the Movement and two other dignitaries who had come from Vlodrop, were in the air above the Ardennes, enjoying the fabulous view. It was indeed a pure gift, because nothing ever came out of the project.

Back near Maharishi again

On May 8, 1997, Maharishi wanted to move to his new home, the large Sthapatya Veda house next to the monastery. We Purushas had not been invited to this important event. Nevertheless, four of us went there, from Wavre, on our own initiative and with a somewhat bad conscience. However, we arrived too late to witness the actual Vedic celebration of the move. Nevertheless, we enjoyed the atmosphere of silence, strength and order that prevailed, as always, in Maharishi's vicinity and which now seemed to have increased considerably due to the changed architectural geometry throughout the entire area.

The desire to live in Vlodrop again grew in me. And indeed, only a few days or weeks later, we received the news that some buddy-couples should move to Vlodrop to work on a project there. My buddy Peter and I applied. One morning, while still in meditation, I was informed that Peter and I should come. I sneaked

into the flying room and brought Peter out with some trouble by whispering him out of transcendence. We quickly packed our belongings in suitcases and boxes and headed for Vlodrop.

Here, to our surprise, our group – we were perhaps ten pairs of buddies – received a very privileged activity: each of us was given a small table and a laptop on the ground floor of Maharishi's new house, where otherwise only very few were allowed to enter. Every afternoon, (in the morning we were supposed to meditate), we proudly passed the guards who protected Maharishi's fenced area with our special pass. Afterwards we could play on our computers in the sacred atmosphere of the house, directly under Maharishi's private rooms.

Officially, it was our job to look after other Purusha teams who were active for the Movement somewhere in the world. I decided to simply transfer data concerning 'my' time zone from the Europa-Yearbook to the computer. This was probably the most useful thing I could do, because it meant that I was dealing with these countries, and I hoped that in this way I would have some effect of awareness on the geographical areas and support the teams there. Maharishi hardly cared about us. Only very rarely could I see him walk past the far end of the porch.

One evening, when we were all in the monastery building, he called all the Purusha members to his house for a meeting. I noticed it relatively late and was one of the last to arrive. Maharishi was already there and talking to the men. I could only find one place on the porch to get situated. I could barely see because of a houseplant. I knew it was no accident. Before, I'd always sat in the front row; now I was only on the edge. It was a slight pain once again.

I still did not understand what was going on. My impression was: 'I just have to get through this depression; maybe better times will come again.' I should have known long ago, through the practical wisdom I had absorbed from Maharishi and also through my own experiences, that I was running after a 'mirage', (Fata Morgana) (a word Maharishi used in many situations). Today I am still surprised that I was allowed to join the preferred group in Vlodrop at all.

This pleasant time passed all too quickly. Soon the whole European Purusha was to go to America. There, in the forests near Boone, North Carolina, an American 'Continental Capital' with many Sthapatya Veda houses had just been built. It lay lonely in the mountain forests of that state. Here we were supposed to live and create coherence for North America. But since my mother was not well at that time, I was allowed to stay in Vlodrop for a while and thus within her easy reach. Almost all the others left for America before Guru Purnima. For some months, I got even smaller jobs in Vlodrop, partly in Maharishi's garden. Then, it was time for me to say goodbye. All the rest of Purusha moved to a place near Enschede in Holland.

Detachment from the TM-Movement

In the forest and meadow landscape near Enschede, our Movement had bought a country house two decades ago and has since used it for administrative purposes. It was a huge villa built around the turn of the century with marble flooring, fireplace, wood paneling and Delft tiles, surrounded by a large park that belonged 'to us', with large trees and wildlife.

Here I spent a time that every inhabitant of the earth can only dream of. Our small group of friends, who got along well, just lived for the day. We ate together in the fireplace room and went for walks in the park. From time to time, we drove to Enschede or Gronau to buy food. There was nothing to do but meditate and enjoy. But the strange thing was that I became increasingly unhappy. I did not understand it at first. What more did I want? But the fact was that I was suffering. Only very gradually did I realize that hanging around like this without a meaningful task was not for me.

Finally, I flipped a coin. And in doing so, I aligned myself inwardly with Guru Dev, Maharishi's Master: 'Should I grit my teeth and stay, or go?' The answer was, 'No grinding your teeth!' That was a surprise for me. So far, I had always had very good experiences with the coin oracle. And this time, in addition, I had thrown a special coin that had been consecrated in a big ceremony! So, I decided to trust it.

In the following weeks, I phoned meditating friends all over Germany and asked them for a job. Several possibilities arose, but there was nothing I really liked. One day I visited my friend Gisela at the academy in Schledehausen. And then the idea came to me. Why don't I ask for a job in the office of the Vedic Health Centre, which had been established in the buildings of the Academy two months before, at Maharishi's request? And indeed, the director Michael G., who knew me from my time in Munich, immediately reacted positively. 'Yes, they were actually right now looking for someone.' And so, I ended up in the office of the health center. In this way, I experienced a smooth transition into the world of relative activity. I found a job that I enjoyed, where I could live out my management Sanskaras[*30] and where, outside work hours, I was free to do what I wanted. And yet, I remained involved in the TM Movement. I was still 'International Staff' in a sense, so I could feel protected somehow and was familiar with the whole style of thinking and acting.

In the first two months, I familiarized myself with the system of the clinic. Then something happened which was again typical for the style of our Movement and Maharishi's training methods. As soon as I had understood the principles, I suddenly became the administrative head of our whole small special clinic. It started quite harmlessly when Michael called Nandkishore to ask him something. During the conversation, Nandkishore came up with the idea, in the style of Maharishi, to send Michael and his wife to America for three months to familiarize themselves with a new branch of Vedic treatment. In addition, who would take over all their tasks in the meantime? 'Well, Hans, he'll do the job.'

So, there I was the boss, I had four or five telephones on my desk with which I could call Vaidyas[*27], therapists, drivers and patients, back and forth. I also had to write bills, collect money, greet patients, check rooms, sometimes clean up, by myself, and negotiate with Gisela, who was legally the top boss of the whole complex. All in all, I had all-out fun with this work. Such a management job had always been a dream of mine.

But my enthusiasm did not last long. It was just like the last ticking of an old clock. And when my Sanskaras[*30] had expired after about one and a half years, Maharishi promptly had the idea to close down the whole academy in Schledehausen including my department and to tear down the buildings. My assistant Doro and I moved into the TM Academy with a remaining office of the health center at Bremen, in order to care for the former patients from there.

I just said 'promptly', because again and again I had the idea that Maharishi had moved this Vedic health center to Schledehausen because of me. One year later, when I withdrew from it completely in Bremen and officially signed off, it went back almost immediately to where it had been moved from, with a lot of effort, shortly before I arrived in Schledehausen; It went back to Holland.

Besides, the beginning of this whole project was already very interesting, due to unforeseen circumstances I found myself one evening in late summer 1998 very close to the Academy Schledehausen. It was then that I had the idea to stay overnight with Gisela, the always very hospitable director of the academy. When I stood in front of her door at 10 o' clock in the evening, she exclaimed: 'Hans, what are you doing here?' Her second sentence was, 'Imagine, just a minute ago, I hung up the phone. A call had come from International that the Vedic Health Center should be moved here from Holland. What a coincidence! Just a minute ago!'

Gisela then called her two closest colleagues together and told them about the exciting news. During the following discussion, my coming was somehow part of all this revolutionary news for everyone present. At one point, Jürgen, a former member of Purusha, even said, 'Hans, how are you getting involved here now?' He had implied that I was a determined 'lifelong' Purusha member and I replied indignantly: 'Are you crazy! Are you trying to get me off Purusha?'

A few months later, however, I actually was there, i. e. I was 'involved', or rather I had been brought in by Nature or, by Maharishi, as the executive organ of the cosmos? Certainly, Maharishi had killed several birds with the same stone. I don't think it is impossible that I was one of those birds. Quite an effort for a single person like me! But I had already experienced such events several times during my time in Seelisberg.

So, after the closing of Schledehausen I went to Bremen. Apart from the fact that I had less and less fun at my (remaining) job, it became more and more clear to me that Maharishi actually did not guide and lead me anymore, since he had not paid any attention to me at all, when I met him last. I still clung to him as my spiritual teacher. But now I thought: 'Is he still my personal Master, if he doesn't guide me anymore?'

All these thoughts gave me the courage to free myself more and more from him, inwardly. I felt that I no longer needed to follow him in all details. It was really a kind of revolution in my thinking. And it was a great relief. But I also knew that I would be eternally grateful to him for everything he had done for me. In fact, to this day I follow many of his hints and advice, which so often prove to be immensely practical and useful, as they flowed from his immense wisdom. I still feel very connected, infinitely grateful to him.

And so, I gradually cut myself off not only from Maharishi, but also from the whole TM Movement, which had been my spiritual and also physical home for 33 years.

Epilogue

On February 5, 2008, Maharishi has now left his body in Vlodrop. Finally, I went to Vlodrop again, to the residence of Maharishi and Purusha. This time for 'Guru Purnima', the big full moon festival in July. I had not been there for seven years, as I felt that I had not much to do with the 'Movement' anymore. But this time it seemed to me that I should 'say goodbye' to my Purusha friends once again. Saying goodbye was actually the word I had in mind.

At Vlodrop, Maharishi could no longer be seen live. Not since many years. One was lucky to see him on a video transmission, which happened rarely. This time, however, I was lucky, because a short speech to the festival participants was transmitted on large screens into the festival tent. The quality of the transmission was miserable, in contrast to in the olden days. But, it was nice to see a lot of old friends again. I still got along with them on a deep level. Today I am very happy to have been once again in this atmosphere and in Maharishi's proximity.

At the end of the 2007, he announced that he wanted to retire. It was known that he had become very frail in the meantime. He said he would not appear in the video public any more. Maybe he would write another book.

I forgot his birthday on January 12th! When I remembered that, I got a little shock and almost a bad conscience, that such a thing was possible!

Soon afterwards, a friend told me on the phone that Maharishi had left his body two evenings before. At first, I could not talk anymore and had to hang up. I breathed heavily and cried. But strangely enough not for long. After about a day the shock and the pain were gone, I had already experienced my pain of parting many years ago.

Many meditators had travelled to Vlodrop to say goodbye to his body. I knew nothing of this possibility, as I was hardly connected with the Movement anymore. I do not know if I would have gone there either.

But then, recently, something wonderful happened. It was on an evening at my home, in a relatively small group. While my partner, who has mediumistic abilities, gave me a 'Oneness-Blessing', she saw Maharishi and also behind me his Master, Guru Dev. Both took part in the blessing, so to speak. Maharishi also let me know through her that he was grateful for the work I had done for him and that he was sorry for having praised me so little at the time. He said that he would continue to accompany and support me, including in completing this book.

Through all this writing, my love for Maharishi became very much alive again, and I would like to take this opportunity to once again express my deepest gratitude to him for his immeasurable support and encouragement.

Notes and Glossary

1 **Veda** – sanskr. knowledge, the holy scriptures of the old Indian culture

2 **Purusha** – sanskr. Man, human, humanity, person, primal soul

3 **Ayurvedic** – Ayurveda, sanskr. ayu – life, veda – knowledge; collection of the most important textbooks of ancient Indian naturopathy

4 **Jai Guru Dev** – sanskr. Jai (spoken Jay) – expression of praise; Guru – teacher/master; Guru Dev – Maharishi's master

5 **Dhoti** – traditional leg dress of Indian men, adapted to the hot climate,

6 **Mantra** – sanskr. mental tool, a word sound, which is used on the mental level as a meditation vehicle

7 **Badge** – course participant badge

8 **TTC** – Teacher Training Course – TM Teacher Training Course

9 **Lecture** – During a lecture there is normally no meditation, of course, but during the TM mediation you may simultaneously hear what is going on around you and what is being said. So meditating during the lecture was an exceptional situation.

10 **Fiuggi Fonte** – The whole course had moved to Fiuggi near Rome.

11 **Unstressing** – Resolving deep-rooted stress, i. e. tensions, old burdens etc., a kind of 'initial aggravation'.

12 **Sattva** – sanskr. Purity, spiritual power

13 **Puja set** – Puja sanskr. Reverence – an ancient Vedic ritual.

14 **ATR course** – Advanced Training Recourse, advanced training course for TM teachers

15 **Flying Sutra** – sanskr. Sutra – short text formula, proposition

16 **MERU** – Maharishi European Research University, the private research university of TM, which was based in Seelisberg

17 see Youtube: Historical details of increased coherence in the world with Col Gunter Chassé

18 **KSCI** – Channel for SCI, the 'Science of Creative Intelligence'

19 **Pandit disciples** – Pandit sanskr. brahmanic scholar

20 **Mahalakshmi** – sanskr. maha great, lakschmi happiness; goddess of wealth and abundance; Hindu deities do not represent individuals but aspects of the one, all-encompassing deity

21 **Bhajans** – devotional chants

22 **Rudraksha chain** – Indian prayer chain, also called 'Mala', comparable to the Catholic rosary, usually consisting of 108 'Rudrakshas', dried and supposedly especially healing fruits of the Rudraksha tree.

23 **Lingam** – sanskr. Mark, limb. 'Shiva' means in Sanskrit 'the kind,' 'the gracious,' or 'the friend. As part of the Hindu Trinity (Trimurti) with the three aspects Brahma, the Creator, and Vishnu, the Preserver, Shiva embodies the principle of destruction. Since the Divine is formless, Shiva is rarely worshipped in anthropomorphic form, but mainly in its emblem, an egg-shaped phallic symbol, the lingam.

24 **Kurta** – simple traditional long shirt made of cotton, which is widespread in large parts of South Asia.

25 **Swami** – sanskr. owner, lord, master; a Hindu monk

26 **pooh**! – Because of thieves and robbers, trains in India are usually locked from the inside at night.

27 **Vaidya** – Ayurvedic doctor

28 **Rigveda** – the oldest surviving testimony of Indo-European language and culture

29 **Carnet** – French booklet; customs permit for import and export of goods

30 **Sanskaras** – sanskr. hidden, unfulfilled wishes and tendencies, possibly from past lives

31 **Kabbalah** – Hebrew: the traditional Jewish secret doctrine that works strongly with the interpretation of letters and numbers

32 **Shankara** – sanskr. redeemer; one of the most important religious teachers and new founders of Hinduism (ca. 788 – 820)

Helena Olson: His Holiness Maharishi Mahesh Yogi: A Living Saint for the New Millennium Stories of His First Visit to the USA

When Maharishi arrived in Los Angeles in 1959, subjects such as Ayurveda, Gandharva-Veda, Jyotish, meditation, Vastu, Yagya or Yoga were still hardly known in the West. His life's work was to bring the scattered Vedic knowledge into a holistic system of Vedic Science and to make it available for modern man. In May 1959 he brought the subject of meditation to Hollywood's Masquers Club.

Helena and Roland Olson were also in the audience at that time. They are thrilled! They invite him to their house for a week, but a week turns into a whole summer. Because soon all the threads come together in their house. From here the Transcendental Meditation movement spreads quickly throughout the western world. The amusing and sometimes quite delicate daily occurrences, the view of a charming personality and the desire to share Maharishi's words of wisdom with others prompted Helena Olson to tell the story of Maharishi's early days in the West.

250 pages with many historic photos
Paperback ISBN 978-8178222172
Hardcover ISBN 978-1929297214

9 783945 004470